The stranger's dark eyes burned into hers. Jessica was almost gasping for air; her skin was tingling all over. Where his arms held her her skin felt on fire. "Jessica," he said hoarsely.

"Yes," she answered, not caring what the question was. She leaned closer to him again for another kiss, but suddenly he was on his feet, staring down at her.

"Jessica—I'm sorry," he said. He raked a hand through his honey-colored hair. "Jessica—I can't."

"Can't what?" she asked. An icy sensation coiled itself in her stomach. "You know we're supposed to be together. You know it."

"Maybe we— No. We don't know that. We just met. I'm sorry, Jessica. We can't be together. I can't—I can't ever see you again." He took one of her hands and pressed a searing kiss into her palm before turning and striding quickly away from her across the sand.

JESSICA'S
SECRET LOVE

Written by
Kate William

Created by
FRANCINE PASCAL

BANTAM BOOKS
NEW YORK · TORONTO · LONDON · SYDNEY · AUCKLAND

RL 6, age 12 and up

JESSICA'S SECRET LOVE
A Bantam Book / July 1994

Sweet Valley High® is a registered trademark of Francine Pascal
Conceived by Francine Pascal
Produced by Daniel Weiss Associates, Inc.
33 West 17th Street
New York, NY 10011
Cover art by Bruce Emmett

ISBN: 0-553-56229-0

Published simultaneously in the United States and Canada

Bantam Books are published by Bantam Books, a division of Bantam
Doubleday Dell Publishing Group, Inc. Its trademark, consisting of the
words "Bantam Books" and the portrayal of a rooster, is Registered in
U.S. Patent and Trademark Office and in other countries. Marca
Registrada. Bantam Books, 1540 Broadway, New York, New York 10036.

PRINTED IN THE UNITED STATES OF AMERICA

OPM   0 9 8 7 6 5 4 3 2 1

Chapter 1

"Pass me the sunscreen, please," Jessica Wakefield said to her best friend, Lila Fowler. They, along with Jessica's twin sister, Elizabeth, and Elizabeth's best friend, Enid Rollins, were spending the hot Tuesday morning at the Sweet Valley beach. The summer sun was almost too much to take.

"Since when do you use sunscreen?" Lila asked in disbelief, passing Jessica the bottle. Jessica started slathering the cream lavishly over her darkly tanned legs.

"Since we got back from England," Jessica said. "Tans weren't the thing over there—the paler-than-pale look is in. It looked kind of romantic. Kind of European. I thought I'd try lightening up a bit."

Elizabeth smiled and put down the book she was reading. "It's true. So many women there had

1

beautiful peaches-and-cream complexions. But trust Jessica to use sunscreen for beauty purposes instead of health reasons!"

"Well, some of us take pride in our appearance," Jessica said smugly, admiring her long legs. "And rightly so."

Elizabeth tossed a handful of warm sand onto her bare feet.

"Hey! That stuff burns my dainty feet," Jessica said in mock outrage.

"Well," Elizabeth joked, "I wouldn't want them to get too much of this damaging California sun. I'm just trying to protect their European pallor."

Jessica and Elizabeth enjoyed being the only set of identical twins at Sweet Valley High. At sixteen, they each had long, sunstreaked blond hair, blue-green eyes, and identical dimples in their left cheeks. They also had slim, athletic figures, but that's where their similarities ended.

"I know you guys got all mixed up with that psycho who thought he was a werewolf—but did you manage to have any fun at all?" Enid asked. "Or was it just work, work, work at your London newspaper internship?"

Elizabeth forced a smile. She hadn't had a chance to tell Enid the whole sordid story, and if she were honest with herself, she knew that part of her was still pretty confused and embarrassed about what had happened. During their month in England, they had served as cub reporters for the

2

London Journal. Although for a while it had looked as if they each found a romantic Englishman to fall in love with, Elizabeth's had turned out to be a serial killer. She was still having nightmares about it.

"It was pretty much mostly work. I learned a lot about police procedure," Elizabeth said tightly.

"It's too bad that Todd left just as you got back," Enid sympathized.

Elizabeth nodded and rolled onto her back, holding her book above her to keep the sun out of her eyes. "Yeah. Though in a way, I don't mind having the break—I don't really feel like being with anyone right now."

Enid nodded, a look of concern crossing her face.

"When's Todd coming back?" Jessica asked her sister.

"A little over two weeks. His family went to visit his grandmother, as they do every summer."

"Well, you have two whole weeks to get yourself together," Jessica said cheerfully. "In the meantime, what could be better after all that London drizzle than good old California sunshine?"

Elizabeth smiled faintly. "You're right, Jess. It's good to be home."

"Speaking of getting yourself together, I feel as if I need a little exercise. Lila, care to join me in a quick jog along the water?"

Lila wrinkled her nose. "Ugh. It's too hot. I think I'll just stay here and take a nap."

Jessica gave Lila a meaningful look. "*Li*la. I said, let's go for a little *jog*." Jessica felt sorry for her sister, but listening to Elizabeth's boring theories about what went wrong in London didn't really figure into her plans for her first day back on the beach.

"Jessica, I said—oh, right. Sure, I'd love to go for a jog." She turned to Elizabeth and Enid. "Will you guys watch our stuff till we get back?"

"Of course," Enid agreed, and Jessica and Lila got up and headed down the white sand toward the water.

"What was that about?" Elizabeth murmured, squinting up at Enid.

"No idea. Guess they just want to gossip without us."

Elizabeth giggled. "They'll never change. It's comforting, somehow."

"I know what you mean. Boy, it sure is good to have you home, Liz. Going to the Dairi Burger wasn't the same without you."

"Thanks, Enid. I missed you, too. It seems as though everywhere I went I saw things I wanted to show you or tell you about. We'll have to go there together someday."

Enid nodded enthusiastically. "Maybe for our junior year abroad in college," she suggested. "Or we could go there one summer between semesters."

"Hmmm. That sounds good. But for right now, I just want to enjoy being home."

"What happened exactly, Liz? I mean, you've given me the general outline, but I still don't understand the whole picture. If you're OK talking to me about it, that is," she added quickly.

"You know I feel as if I can tell you anything, Enid—it's just that I want to put it behind me." Elizabeth sighed and took a long drink of her fruit juice. "Basically, what happened was that I met this romantic, sweet, unassuming guy, and suddenly I thought he was meant for me, you know? In a different way than Todd. I sort of let myself get carried away by the fact that he was a poet and all. And we really seemed to be on the same wavelength. But if we were so close, why couldn't I pick up on any of his tortured feelings beneath the surface? Now I feel weird inside, as though I can't trust my instincts. Can't trust guys. I just can't believe I made such a huge mistake."

"I understand," Enid said. "But you can trust Todd, can't you?"

"Enid, right now I feel as though I can't even trust myself." Elizabeth lay back on her towel and picked up her book again, aware of her friend's concerned gaze.

"OK, we're out of sight. Can we stop jogging now? I have a stitch," Lila panted. "Now, what's up?"

The two girls slowed to a leisurely walk, and Jessica glanced back to make sure her sister was nowhere around. She looked over at Lila, whose face was flushed and damp with heat.

"Speaking of getting in shape . . ." she said teasingly.

"Oh, shut up. You know I get plenty of exercise," Lila said huffily. "I must have gone around the entire mall *twice* yesterday, looking for a new pair of sandals."

"Well, the only exercise I've had recently is rescuing my naive sister from maniacs in London." Jessica shivered, despite the sun's warmth. "No kidding, Li—she was pretty hooked on Luke. Ever since we got back, she's been moping around, saying she'll never trust anyone again, that there must be something wrong with her to have been attracted to him. I mean, I see her point, but *yawn*."

"There *is* something wrong with her. She's been with Todd Wilkins too long," Lila stated, scuffling her bare feet in the sand. "What a drip. Hey, I read that walking barefoot in sand acts as a natural skin buffer, smoothing away any rough spots."

"Really?" Jessica started scuffling her feet too, trying to feel the natural sloughing action. "And it's not just her, Lila. It's me, too. I mean, I had a great time with Lord Robert—you should have heard his sexy English accent. I could have sat and listened to him read the phone book, you know? But that's just it—he lives in England, and we knew from the beginning it wouldn't go anywhere. I'm ready to meet someone new—someone who really blows me away." She looked out over the waves. "After

6

Sam died, I thought I'd never want to get close to anyone again. But now I feel—I don't know. That it's time to go on."

Jessica's only serious boyfriend had been killed in a tragic car accident several months before.

"Good for you, Jess," Lila said. "Life is for the living, that's what I say. You've been really brave, and really strong, and I think it's great that you're ready to move on and meet some new eligible stud."

Jessica smiled at her friend. "Thanks, Li."

"Could you just please make sure that your hunk has a gorgeous brother or friend? I need someone new too. I've been doing a lot of thinking while you were gone—"

"Whoa. You *must* have been bored," Jessica interrupted teasingly.

"*As* I was saying," Lila continued, "I've decided to turn over a new leaf. This social-butterfly business is getting a little old. I want to find one totally fantastic guy and see only him. The problem is finding a guy who could actually keep me interested for more than three days." She sighed.

"That's always the problem," Jessica agreed. "Gosh, can you believe this heat? Let's run for a while along the water." She broke into an easy jog, splashing through the very edge of the surf, her long blond hair streaming out behind her.

"*Jess*," Lila groaned, but she began to run after her. "Wait up!"

7

"Last one to the point is a rotten—Ow!" A white Frisbee suddenly came out of nowhere and sailed right into Jessica's head, hard. Startled, Jessica clapped a hand to her head and stumbled, falling to her knees in the shallow surf of the ocean.

Lila trotted up beside her. "Are you OK?" Lila asked, panting and out of breath. "What jerk threw that thing? Let me see your head. It doesn't look like you're bleeding."

"Maybe *I'm* not bleeding," Jessica snarled, "but the idiot who owns that Frisbee is going to be, as soon as I lay my hands on him. Or her." She rubbed the spot where the Frisbee had whacked her.

Lila looked around. "I don't see anyone..... Oh."

Jessica looked up through her hair to see a guy sprinting toward her across the sand and her heart constricted painfully.

"Whoa," Lila murmured softly. "He is *hot*."

"Hot" didn't begin to describe the gorgeous guy headed their way. As Jessica gazed at this bronzed Greek god in black swim trunks, his broad, tan shoulders, his muscled arms, her heart slowed to a dull thud. "Who is that?" she choked out.

"He must be new around here. I'm sure I'd remember if I'd ever seen *him* before."

Then the stranger was there, kneeling beside Jessica and putting a warm hand on her bare shoulder. "Oh, wow, I'm sorry," he said in a rich, husky voice. "The wind caught the Frisbee and slammed

8

it into you. I'm really sorry. Are you all right?"

He was even more gorgeous up close, the most gorgeous guy Jessica had ever seen, heard, thought of, or stood next to in her entire life. She looked up into dark-brown eyes the color of coffee, at his thick, wavy honey-blond hair, damp from the saltwater. His nose was straight, his chin firm. And he was older, maybe college-age.

"Miss?" He was searching her face in concern, and Jessica realized she hadn't spoken yet.

"I'm OK," she said, lowering her voice so that it wouldn't tremble.

"Can you stand up? Let me help you." As the beautiful golden guy put a strong arm around her back to help her stand, Jessica's knees felt even weaker from his touch. She dug her toes into the wet sand and willed herself to stand up straight. She could feel the heat radiating off of him, as though he were made of sunlight itself.

"Let's see, where did it hit you?" he murmured, his fingers roving over the side of her head, sending tingles down Jessica's spine.

"Right here." Jessica pointed to the tender bump that was forming. She brushed away her bangs, which covered half her face.

"Hmm. We should get you—" The stranger broke off with a start upon looking at her face more closely, seeing her clearly for the first time, "—some ice."

He stepped back a little, though his hand re-

9

mained tangled in her sea-damp blond hair. For long moments they stood staring at each other, and Jessica's bruised skin tingled beneath his touch. *He's my soul mate, the one I've always dreamed of, the one I've been waiting for,* she thought. *This was meant to be.* She knew it as clearly and sharply and definitely as her own name.

"Uh, you'd better sit down for a moment," the stranger said.

He looked pale beneath his tan and shaken as he led her over to a wooden beach lounger with an umbrella. Once there, he sank down instantly, as though his knees were as weak as hers. His hand, still entwined with hers, pulled her down next to him. Jessica looked down at their knees, almost touching, and her heart suddenly started beating hard again, as though it had been jump started.

"So, Jess, are you OK?" Lila asked, standing in front of her.

"Oh—Lila." She'd forgotten that Lila was with her, that anyone but this golden stranger existed. "I'm . . . fine," she said firmly, and gave Lila a bright smile. "I'm fine," she repeated, turning to smile at the stranger. She was pleased to hear her voice sound almost normal.

"Wow, are you all right?"

Jessica glanced up to see another boy looking at her with concern. Not a boy, she amended. He was a little older too. She saw Lila's eyes lock on him like a cat on a catnip mouse.

10

"Sorry about that," he said. "That was my throw. I didn't know old fumble fingers here would miss it."

"The wind took it," the blond stranger said.

"It's OK. No harm done," Jessica told the dark-haired boy. *No harm at all.*

"Good," he said cheerfully. He turned to Lila and held out his hand. "Robby Goodman. Pleased to meet you."

Lila laughed and flicked her long brown hair over her shoulder. "Lila Fowler." They shook hands, and then he smiled at Jessica expectantly.

"Jessica," she said.

"Jessica," the blond boy said softly, his dark eyes locking onto hers. She shivered. Coming from him, her name sounded like music.

"Well, hey. How about I buy you guys a soda, sort of make up for bonking you with the Frisbee," Robby offered.

"That would be great," Lila said. "I'll go with you."

Jessica shook her head. "I don't need one, thanks." She felt the stranger's hand tighten around hers.

"No thanks, Robby. You go ahead," he said.

"OK. Catch you later," Robby said, and turned to walk up the beach to the soda stand.

"I'll be back soon, Jess," Lila said. "Maybe." She winked at Jessica, then followed Robby across the white sand.

"Are you sure you're OK?" the stranger asked Jessica when they were alone again. He looked deeply into her blue-green eyes.

11

Jessica nodded, drinking in every detail of his face, his blond hair, the smiling glints in his dark eyes.

"You're so beautiful," he blurted suddenly. "I never thought—" He stopped and turned away, looking toward the ocean, where the waves were tumbling gently against the sand. "I mean, I didn't expect—" He broke off again, not looking at her.

"Me neither," Jessica said softly. "I never expected to meet someone like you."

When the the stranger turned back to her, he looked upset, almost angry, Jessica realized. Was it only about the Frisbee, or was it something else?

"Exactly," he said. Pain lined his face even as his hand came up and gently stroked the smooth tan skin of her shoulder. Jessica could feel the flare of appreciation in his warm gaze. "I never expected to meet you—not now," he agreed bleakly.

"Why not now?" Jessica asked softly, leaning a little closer to him. "It feels so . . . right. It feels like fate."

He looked at her with an intensity she found almost frightening. "Maybe it is," he murmured, lowering his head and claiming her lips in a kiss.

Jessica gently touched his face and neck as she edged closer to him. Her feelings for young Lord Robert Pembroke in London suddenly seemed insignificant. *I haven't felt like this since Sam,* Jessica realized instantly. And now, for the first time in the long months since Sam Woodruff had died, the sun had come out. This stranger's kiss had healed the pain.

The golden head pulled away, and dark eyes burned into hers. Jessica was almost gasping for air; her skin was tingling all over. Where his arms held her her skin felt on fire. "Jessica," he said hoarsely.

"Yes," she answered, not caring what the question was. She leaned closer to him again for another kiss, but suddenly he was on his feet, staring down at her.

"Jessica—I'm sorry," he said. He raked a hand through his honey-colored hair. "Jessica—I can't."

"Can't what?" she asked. An icy sensation coiled itself in her stomach. "You know we're supposed to be together. You know it."

"Maybe we— No. We don't know that. We just met. I'm sorry, Jessica. We can't be together. I can't—I can't ever see you again." He took one of her hands and pressed a searing kiss into her palm before turning and striding quickly away from her across the sand.

Jessica sat frozen on the beach chair, as though she'd been struck. *What are you doing? Run after him,* a part of her cried out. But something stopped her. *His eyes looked so . . . tortured.* He'd meant what he'd said. Whatever his reasons, they couldn't be together. For the second time in her life, Jessica felt her heart break.

Chapter 2

"Well, this experience with Luke has taught me one thing," Elizabeth said to Enid when they'd come back to their towels after a quick swim. "I definitely have some issues I need to work on. For one thing, I need to understand myself more, my motivations. For another thing, I suddenly feel as if I don't have a handle on romantic relationships. But this book I've been reading is a start." She held up her thick, oversized paperback.

"*Real Women, Bad Men*," Enid read the title. "What's it about?"

"It's about why we get involved in unhealthy relationships. The author gives examples of different kinds of behavior patterns, and there are little quizzes at the end of each chapter to see if you have any of them. Then she explains how these patterns affect your relationships."

"That sounds really, um, interesting," Enid, said, looking skeptical.

"Yeah, it is. I really recommend it. I've already learned some stuff about how Todd and I interact. And it's pointed out a few things about why I was attracted to Luke."

"Well, as long as it's helping," Enid said, pushing her sunglasses up on her nose. "Maybe I'll read it when you're finished."

"Hey, guys." Jessica trudged up to them across the sand. Her hair was dripping and her bathing suit was wet. "The water feels great," she said morosely.

Elizabeth looked up from her book. "What's the matter? You look bummed. Where's Lila?"

"Lila met a hunk and went off with him." Jessica flopped down on her towel on her stomach and rested her head on her hands.

"Jessica, what's wrong?" Elizabeth persisted. As always, Elizabeth could read her sister's mood in a second.

"I just met the most wonderful guy in the world," Jessica moaned. "That's what's wrong!"

"*Oh*," said Elizabeth, laughing in relief. Jessica met a new wonderful guy practically every week. "So where is he?"

"Don't ask. He was fabulous, Liz. More than fabulous. As soon as we met, something clicked. And I could tell it was like that for him, too. It was as if we had always known each other. But then out of nowhere he jumped up, said we couldn't see

16

each other anymore, and ran off. Leaving me alone and brokenhearted," Jessica finished dramatically.

Elizabeth and Enid exchanged glances. "So let's get this straight," Elizabeth said in a businesslike tone. "You met, it was love at first sight, and he left? That's the whole story?"

"Uh-huh." Jessica closed her eyes.

"Well, maybe your radiance was too much to take in a large dose," Elizabeth said. "He'll probably come crawling back as soon as he cools off, since you're the love of his life and all."

Enid stifled a giggle behind her hand.

Jessica sat up, her eyes blazing. "Liz! I'm serious! This was the man I was supposed to marry, and now he's gone. I'm destined to be an old maid forever now. It isn't funny."

"I'm only kidding, Jess," Elizabeth protested. "I really do think he'll be back sometime. What was his name?"

"I don't know," Jessica admitted. "But I know that we were meant to be together."

"Uh-huh. And how many times have I heard that?" Elizabeth said playfully. "How about two weeks ago, with Lord Robert? It says right here in this book that falling in love all the time is a symptom of low self—"

"Liz, for your information, Robert was just a holiday fling. This is the real thing. Not even Sam made me feel this way."

Elizabeth gazed at Jessica in shock, her book slipping from her hand. Enid's mouth dropped open.

Before they could speak, Jessica gathered up her belongings into an untidy lump. "I have to get out of here. I want to go home. Are you coming?"

"Sure, I'll come with you," Elizabeth managed to get out. "Just hang on a minute." Jessica stalked away toward the parking lot, and Elizabeth got her things together.

"Wow," Enid said in an awed tone. "I can't believe she said that. She adored Sam."

"I know. It's really weird. It's a good thing I'm reading this book—maybe I can help her sort out her feelings. I'll talk to you later."

Elizabeth started to run across the sand after Jessica, her arms full of her towel, her mini-cooler, and her thick book. "Jess, wait up!"

As they drove home in the black Jeep that they shared, Elizabeth darted concerned glances at Jessica. "Are you OK?" she said finally.

Jessica sighed. "Yeah. I'm sorry I snapped at you on the beach. It's just that I feel so weird about this guy."

"Jess," Elizabeth said gently, "I learned the hard way in England that even when you think you know someone, you might not, really. After all, you don't even know this boy's name."

"He's not a boy—he's a man. He's older than us by a couple of years, I think. I know you're still shaken up by that crazy Luke, but this is different,

Liz. When he kissed me it was as if—"

"You kissed him?" Elizabeth practically shrieked. "Jessica, are you crazy? Can't you learn from my bad example? You can't go around kissing total strangers!"

"I keep telling you, Liz. He wasn't a stranger. He was my dream guy, the guy I never thought existed." Jessica looked at the passing scenery as Elizabeth headed the Jeep toward Calico Drive, where they lived. Elizabeth gave her a worried glance, but didn't say anything more.

At home Jessica showered and changed into black shorts and a hot-pink tank top, then flopped on her bed. In her mind she replayed every instant of the meeting with her dream man over and over again. Her skin tingled and she wrapped her arms around herself as she remembered their kiss. Then she pulled back and pictured his eyes, so dark, so full of unexpressed emotion. *"Not now,"* she heard him say again, and shivered. Did he have some terrible secret?

The telephone rang, and Jessica jumped. *He's found my number. He's changed his mind,* she thought for one split second. After all, he knew her name. Her first name anyway.

"Jessica! Phone for you," Elizabeth called. Jessica leaped off her bed and sprinted into the hall. Her heart pounding, she picked up the extension and heard Elizabeth hang up the other phone.

19

"Hello?" she said breathlessly. *Please, oh, please* . . .

"Jess? Li. You'll never believe what happened. Talk about a match made in heaven," Lila gloated.

"Oh, hi, Lila," Jessica said, carrying the phone into her room. She pushed some dirty laundry aside with her foot and made her way back to her bed.

"Well, don't act too excited to hear from me," Lila said sarcastically. "Never mind, I'll forgive you. Jess, Robby is the most amazing guy. You won't believe how well-suited we are. This is it, I'm telling you. He's the one. And we have a date for tonight, too."

"Tonight?" Jessica repeated.

"Sure. What's wrong with tonight?" Lila asked. "The best part is, he's of my social strata. I'm not a snob or anything, but it's just so much easier to talk to someone when they know where St. Moritz is."

"Oh, definitely," Jessica said, rolling her eyes. "I've always said so. So how could you tell he's rich? Was he wearing a gold-plated swimsuit?"

"No," Lila said with exaggerated patience. "He was wearing a gold *watch*. And not plated, either. And he drives a Lamborghini. And he has the most adorable little Scottie. I just love expensive dogs, don't you?"

"Wow," Jessica said. Lucky Lila. She had her dream guy, while Jessica had only a broken heart.

"Uh-huh," Lila said happily. "It was parked right next to my Triumph in the parking lot. Like it was fate or something."

"Yeah, fate or something," Jessica parroted

absentmindedly. Then a thought occurred to her. "Say, did he mention anything about his friend?"

"Yeah, what's-his-name."

"Uh-huh?" Jessica said eagerly.

"No, I mean, what *is* his name, Jess?"

"I don't know," Jessica had to admit. "We never got around to that."

"Hmmm. I guess you had better things to do." Lila laughed knowingly. "But you'll find out when he calls you, right?"

"He's not going to call." Jessica filled Lila in on the whole heartbreaking story.

"How weird," Lila said when Jessica was done. "I guess *I* know more about him than you do."

"Tell me everything Robby said about him," Jessica begged.

"He said that his friend was staying with him while he was in town on business, and that they had gone to college together. I think your mystery man is from the northeast somewhere—maybe Boston or New York. Let me think."

Jessica paced her room anxiously while she waited for Lila to remember more. Boston or New York? She imagined herself walking the streets of the two major cities, searching for a blond Adonis. Where would she start?

"He works for some nature organization. Yeah, that's it. Robby said his friend was a real conservation nut, very dedicated to his job." Lila paused.

"Come to think of it, Jess, Robby did say something odd about him."

"What? What?"

"Well, I was just joking around, and I said something like, 'You two are best friends, and Jessica and I are best friends. Maybe we'll all double date or something.' You know. And he suddenly looked serious, and said something like, 'Maybe Jessica should just forget she ever met him.' Or something like that. That you should just forget him."

"I don't get any of this. What's the big mystery? Oh, Lila, this is going to make me crazy!"

"Hmmm, maybe they're spies or something." Lila laughed. "Listen—I'm seeing Robby tonight. I'll try to pump him for information, OK?"

"Oh, thanks, Li. You're a real friend," Jessica said gratefully. "Find out his name, where he lives, anything."

"I'll try, though I have to warn you—I'm sure Robby and I will be talking mostly about ourselves!" She laughed again.

Jessica smiled wrly into the phone. Of course! Lila Fowler's favorite subject was Lila Fowler. "Anyway, thanks, Li. Have a good time."

A conservation nut, Jessica thought after they hung up. *How sexy.* Jessica threw herself back on her bed and pictured her mystery man slashing his way through a jungle, on his way to stop some illegal lumber company from stealing trees from the rain forest. She was beside him, wearing a really cute safari outfit that showed off her legs.

"I got an interesting letter today," Mrs. Wakefield told her family that night at dinner. "From Sue Gibbons. Nancy's daughter."

Elizabeth looked at her mother with concern. Nancy Marest Gibbons had been Alice Wakefield's college roommate and had died not too long ago. Alice had cried for three days straight, saying that Nancy had been like a sister to her.

"What did she say, Mom?" Elizabeth asked gently.

"Well, she wrote to tell me that she's engaged and she's always wanted a California wedding, just like her mother had. She was asking for my advice." Mrs. Wakefield helped herself to some salad and continued. "I was thinking, instead of just giving her advice, I'd like to ask her to come stay here with us while she plans the wedding. In a way, I feel I owe it to Nancy—and I feel bad that Sue doesn't have a mother to help her at such an important time. What does everybody think?"

"That's really nice of you, Mom. It sounds like fun," Elizabeth said enthusiastically, thinking that being able to help Nancy's daughter would help Alice get through her grief. "I love weddings. But isn't eighteen awfully young to be getting married?"

Mrs. Wakefield nodded. "I imagine that, because of her mother's illness and untimely death, Sue's probably feeling a little lost. One way for her to feel secure again would be to get married and have her own family. Of course, I'm just guessing."

"When would she come, and when would the wedding be?" Jessica asked, interested despite her preoccupation. Maybe planning a wedding would be just what she needed to take her mind off her mystery man. If anything could.

Alice Wakefield smiled at her twin daughters. "She would come in a few days, and I guess it would take almost a month to get the wedding organized. Her stepfather would fly down right before the wedding and stay in a hotel. So what do you say, girls? Shall I call her and tell her it's OK?"

"Yeah," Elizabeth said, thinking it would be good for her mother, and good for her to see a healthy, committed relationship. "Tell her to come."

"I think it's a good idea, Mom," Jessica agreed.

"You're the boss," was Mr. Wakefield's vote.

"Good. I'll call her tonight," Mrs. Wakefield said.

Chapter 3

"Look, girls. I think that's her." Mrs. Wakefield pointed to a dark-haired girl in the middle of the crowd. It was Friday morning and they were at the airport to pick up Sue.

She looks so young to be getting married, Elizabeth thought as she watched the girl with dark, wavy shoulder-length hair came closer. She was very pretty, although Elizabeth thought she detected a slightly forlorn air about her.

When Sue saw the Wakefields, a smile lit up her pretty face, making her appear a little older. "Aunt Alice?" she asked hesitantly.

"Yes, my dear." Mrs. Wakefield stepped closer to her and enfolded her in a warm hug. "How was your flight? Goodness, you've grown up to be a lovely young woman. You look just like your mother did at your age." The girl's warm brown eyes shone back at her.

"Sue, do you remember my husband, Ned? And this is Jessica and Elizabeth. You all were very young the last time you saw one another."

"Sue, glad to have you stay with us," Mr. Wakefield said, shaking her hand.

"Hi, Sue. Welcome to Sweet Valley." Elizabeth gave the older girl a broad smile.

"We can't wait to hear your plans for the wedding," Jessica said. "And we can't wait to show you all the hottest spots in Sweet Valley!" Even though Jessica wanted to be friendly to Sue, she couldn't help feeling a twinge of jealousy—here this girl was just a little older than Jessica, and already planning the rest of her life with her husband.

Sue Gibbons laughed. "That sounds great. I knew I was doing the right thing in coming to Sweet Valley for my wedding."

Elizabeth smiled to herself as she followed her family and Sue through the airport. Sue seemed really nice and down-to-earth. And Jessica seemed to be cheering up. Elizabeth could tell already that Sue's visit would be good for everybody.

By late morning, Ned and Alice Wakefield had seen that Sue was settled, then they headed off for work, leaving Jessica and Elizabeth to entertain their guest.

"So, what should we do first?" Jessica asked. She was lying on her stomach on Steven's bed. Steven, the twins' older brother, was away at college and came home only on weekends sometimes. Sue was going to be staying in his room during her visit.

Sue turned around from where she was hanging up clothes in Steven's closet. Jessica had noticed that Sue's clothes were the latest in New York chic. "I'm completely open to suggestions," she said cheerfully. "I'm sure you two know the best things to do." She shut the closet door and came to sit beside Jessica on the bed. "If it's OK with you guys, I thought maybe the first day or two we should just hang out, and you can show me all the highlights of Sweet Valley. Then we can settle down and really start planning the wedding. I'm depending on you both to help me figure out what to do. I mean," she said with a laugh, "I've never gotten married before!"

Elizabeth came over to pat Sue on the shoulder. "We helped plan our next-door neighbor's wedding not too long ago," Elizabeth said, referring to when Mona Whitman had gotten married, "so we'll put our heads together and come up with something really special for you."

"Thanks," Sue said warmly. "Jeremy—my fiancé—and I really appreciate it. He was so glad to hear I'd have help doing this." Her face clouded over for a moment. "It's kind of hard, not having my mother with me for my wedding. I have some good friends in New York, but they can't really help me from three thousand miles away. So you

27

two and Aunt Alice are real lifesavers."

"We're glad to do it," Elizabeth said. "Now, Jess—what should our first stop be? The beach, the mall, Dairi Burger?"

"It's almost lunchtime, so let's hit the Dairi Burger," Jessica decided.

"Lead the way!" Sue said, laughing.

The next few days passed in a whirlwind. Even Jessica cheered up as they showed Sue all their favorite places—Miller's Point, Sweet Valley High School, the Beach Cafe, Guido's Pizza Palace, the beach. . . . Sue was definitely fun to have around, Jessica decided. She liked to do pretty much the same things the twins did, and wasn't snobby at all. Every once in a while, Jessica had to remind herself that Sue wasn't just another teenager: she was engaged to be married.

On Sunday morning the twins went to the beach with Sue and some of their friends for a little sun and girl talk. Elizabeth and Jessica had different friends and didn't usually end up doing the same things, but they wanted Sue to feel really welcome in Sweet Valley.

"I'm so jealous, Sue," Amy Sutton was saying. She carefully adjusted the straps of her bikini top so that her tan would be even. "You're only eighteen and already getting married. It's so romantic."

Sue smiled without opening her eyes. She was lying on a towel, completely covered in a heavy sunscreen so that she wouldn't be peeling by the wedding. "Well, as soon as I met Jeremy, I knew he was the one for me. It was love at first sight, you know?"

"Yes," Jessica said softly. *All too well . . .*

"As soon as I looked into his eyes, I fell in love, and he says it was the same for him. It was like a force we couldn't control. I mean, finally we decided we had to get married before we got into trouble." Sue blushed and gave a girlish giggle. "He's just the sweetest guy. I like the fact that he's older than me—he's twenty-three. And it really helps that we share our work, too."

"What's your work?" Enid asked.

"We both work at Project Nature in New York."

"Project Nature?" Jessica asked, her heart racing. What if Sue knew her gorgeous stranger?

"Yeah," Sue laughed. "That's where we met, actually. I had decided to take a year off between high school and college, just to get a taste of the real world, you know? So I interned at Project Nature. Jeremy was already working there. He specializes in computer programs that track deforestation around the world. Lately we've been traveling all over together, doing some fund-raising for our cause. We went to New Mexico, and to Michigan. . . ." She sat up suddenly, her unread magazine falling to her side. "It's just so amazing, being with him, being committed to the same thing. I feel as if my whole life is finally falling into place. Right after my mom died, I felt so lost, so

29

alone—even though I still have my stepdad and tons of friends. It's just not the same. But now it seems like heaven to be able to spend the rest of my life with Jeremy, traveling all over the world, trying to educate people to the needs of conservation, doing what little we can to make the world a better place." She looked off into the distance, her love glowing on her face.

"That's terrific," Elizabeth said, putting her hand on Sue's arm. "I know you two are going to be so happy together."

Sue turned to her with a smile. "We already are. Jeremy is everything in the world to me. He's my family, and my future."

Jessica gazed off down the shoreline. Obviously Sue was too caught up in talking about Jeremy to hear Jessica's questions about her dream man. *I can't exactly blame her—she's planning her whole future with the man she loves. But if I don't get a chance to pump her about the man I love, I'll go out of my mind by the end of the day.* She pictured him in the rain forest, looking rugged and passionate.

"Where are you going to register for your wedding?" Lila Fowler asked. "Bibi's is a great place."

Jessica roused herself from her latest safari daydream. "Lila, Bibi's sells mostly jewelry. Sue has to register somewhere where she can get a few practical things, too. You know—blenders, sheets, towels, china. And what about poor Jeremy?"

"I don't know," Sue said with a giggle. "Jewelry

sounds like a great wedding present. Jeremy will just have to get stuck with all the blenders and stuff. It's every man for himself when it comes to the wedding loot. Besides, as he's paying for the wedding, I'm sure he'll be pleased when I make out like a bandit—like we're getting back what he put into it, you know?"

Lila and Amy laughed, but Jessica felt a flicker of surprise. She liked jewelry as much as anyone, but when she thought about weddings she thought of togetherness—not "every man for himself" or "making out like a bandit." She glanced over at Elizabeth, who looked positively shocked.

"Have you thought about the actual wedding at all?" Enid asked.

"I was thinking about having it at the cathedral downtown," Sue said. "It's nice and big, and could hold a lot of people. I'm not sure how many of my friends will come from New York, but I want to be prepared. We could decorate the inside with tons of white flowers, maybe tied with gold ribbon . . . and lots of green leaves and ferns and stuff."

"Sounds fab," Lila said approvingly.

"Wow, it's almost eleven thirty," Elizabeth said, looking at her watch. "Sue, Jess, should we get going to the mall? We can have lunch there."

"Sounds good," Sue said agreeably, standing up and brushing sand off her bathing suit.

"I'm ready," Jessica said. "I'll call you later, Li."

"Yeah, do. I have to give you the next install-

31

ment of 'The Rich and the In Love.'"

"What's that? A new soap?" Enid asked.

Lila laughed and waved one manicured hand. "No—not exactly. But it *is* the story of my life, juicy details, racy love scenes, and all."

Jessica kicked a little sand on Lila as she walked by, and laughing, she, Elizabeth, and Sue headed back to the Jeep.

When Sue skipped a little ahead of the twins in the parking lot, Jessica clutched her sister's arm. "Sue's from New York, and she works as a conservationist," she whispered. "I bet she knows who my guy is!"

"But Jess," Elizabeth whispered back. "You don't even know his name. And you're not even sure he's from New York—it could be Boston, remember? Anyway, there are quite a few conservation groups now—what are the chances of her knowing him, really?"

Jessica gave her sister a sour look. "Thanks for raining on my parade," she said shortly.

"Jess, I don't mean to dash your hopes, but I just want you to be realistic, so you don't get disappointed later. In my book *Real Women, Bad Men*, it said that a major source of frustration for women is unrealistic expectations, especially in relationships. It said—"

"All *right*," Jessica said in as low a voice as she could manage. "You've made your point. Just quit quoting that stupid book at me!"

By the time they reached the Jeep, where Sue stood waiting, it took all Jessica's strength to force her face into a smile.

"I love this mall," Sue said, looking around Sweet Valley's main shopping center. "We don't have anything like this in Manhattan. You have to trudge from one store to the other on the subway. I like this system better, where you just get in your car and drive everywhere."

So much for conserving gas, Elizabeth thought wryly. She liked Sue and was enjoying her visit, but privately she thought Sue seemed a little immature for someone about to get married. *But I'm being too critical of her. It's only natural to joke about your wedding presents, and wish for a life-style that you wouldn't really lead, like driving everywhere.* "It is pretty," she agreed out loud. "I think Jessica knows every square inch of this place—she spends enough time here," she teased her sister.

"Hey, is that plant new?" Jessica stopped dead in her tracks and pointed to a potted mum that was part of a decoration around the center fountain.

Elizabeth giggled. "See what I mean? My sister can even locate every piece of gum stuck to the tables in the food court." The three girls laughed.

"Speaking of the food court, can we have lunch first? I'm starved," Sue said apologetically.

"Lunch first it is," Elizabeth promised.

"How about this burger place?" Sue suggested.

Elizabeth looked at her. The fast-food place in question had had a lot of publicity lately—some rain-forest conservation groups had protested that the company supported slash-and-burn agriculture in South America to raise their beef cattle.

Apparently Sue hadn't heard about it.

"How about the salad bar at the chicken shack?" Elizabeth suggested instead. She was sure Sue wouldn't want to eat at a place other conservationists were boycotting.

"Oh, sure," Sue agreed. "Whatever."

After lunch Jessica and Elizabeth introduced Sue to all their favorite boutiques.

"The best place for clothes is Kiki's," Jessica informed Sue, leading her over to their display window.

"Those leggings are adorable," Sue said.

"You and Jeremy can register at Lytton & Brown," Elizabeth said, naming the area's biggest department store.

"Oh, great. I can't wait for him to get here. I want him to see everything that you've shown me. I'm sure he'll love it as much as I do," Sue said enthusiastically.

"When is he coming?" Elizabeth asked.

"Tomorrow. He had to wrap things up in New York, because we're taking so much time off. But he's had a great idea—there's a branch of Project Nature in Los Angeles. That's only about a half hour away, right?"

"Right," Jessica said.

"Anyway, he thinks we can work there part time while we're in Sweet Valley. It'll make it easier to take off a couple weeks for our honeymoon."

"That's a good plan. Now, do you feel like heading over to Bibi's to look at some engagement rings?" Elizabeth suggested. Sue had told her that she and Jeremy had been so busy in New York that they hadn't gotten a chance to pick out a ring. Elizabeth was planning to take note of the ones Sue liked so that she could tell Jeremy about them later.

"Sounds fine to me." Sue linked arms with both Elizabeth and Jessica, and they headed off to a different wing of the mall.

She's so easygoing, Elizabeth thought. No matter what she and Jessica suggested, Sue always agreed, always seemed cheerful and enthusiastic. Probably Jeremy cherished that aspect of her personality. *Does Todd think of me as easygoing?* Elizabeth mused. *Maybe an easygoing nature is a key ingredient to a strong relationship.* She resolved to look it up in her self-help book when she got home.

"Anyway, we haven't decided where to go for our honeymoon," Sue was chattering on. Her good mood was infectious, and even Jessica looked as though she was having fun talking with Sue.

"Paris would be fabulous," Jessica suggested.

"Oh, can you imagine anything more romantic? There are some fantastic hotels there," Sue exclaimed.

"Jess," Elizabeth chided gently. "Jeremy and Sue probably want to go somewhere where they can do a little fieldwork as well. A couple as committed to their cause as they are wouldn't want to waste time slogging around Paris when they could be educating people in Costa Rica."

"Oh, right, right," Sue said, nodding. "I'll have to ask Jeremy about it. He always has the best ideas." A dreamy smile came over her face. "We want to raise our children with the same beliefs," she said. "That we have to take care of mother earth in order for her to take care of us."

Elizabeth nodded admiringly. "That's beautiful."

"Speaking of beauty, here's Bibi's," Jessica broke in.

Bibi's was one of the more exclusive jewelry stores in Sweet Valley, but they also had some other gift-type items. Lila usually picked out her birthday and Christmas presents from there.

Once inside, the three girls walked from glass case to glass case, examining the gold and silver jewelry. Most pieces were unique, with special designs commissioned by Bibi's and not sold anywhere else.

Elizabeth looked through the case of earrings and found a pair shaped like little silver cats. *Maybe I could hint to Todd about them for my birthday,* she thought. Then she saw their price tag. *So much for that idea.*

Jessica and Sue were already looking at the engagement and wedding ring sets, and Elizabeth wandered over to join them.

"Liz, let's each pick out our favorite ring, just for fun," Jessica suggested.

"OK," Elizabeth agreed. She knew she was still years away from being engaged, but it was fun to look at the rings.

"It's so hard to decide," Sue murmured, examining the case of rings closely. "Sometimes there's a great stone, but its setting is ugly. Or vice versa."

"Mm-hmm," Elizabeth said. "Oh, I think I have mine," she said a minute later. Jessica and Sue both came over to look at her choice. It was a large natural pearl, surrounded by tiny diamonds, on a simple gold band.

"It's pretty," Sue said. "It looks like you."

"It doesn't look much like an engagement ring, though," Jessica commented.

"No," Elizabeth said. "But I like it. That's the one I would pick. How about you guys?"

"I think I found mine over here." Jessica led them to the next case over. "It's that one," she said, tapping gently on the glass top over her ring. Jessica's ring was an oval sapphire, set in a yellow-gold band. It had two small triangular diamonds, one on each side.

"Jessica, that's gorgeous," Elizabeth said. "It's beautiful and classy, just like you." She gave her sister a big smile. Jessica was really being very brave, under the circumstances, Elizabeth thought.

37

Normally, if she were hooked on a guy she couldn't have, everyone would be totally sick of hearing her whining and complaining by now. But she had been on her best behavior since Sue had arrived. Maybe she was growing up.

"It really is nice," Sue said. But then a ring in the counter held her gaze. "Could I try on this one, please?" Sue asked the salesclerk.

The salesclerk took it out and carefully placed it on the ring finger of Sue's left hand.

"I like it," Sue breathed.

"Whoa. It's . . . really something," Jessica said.

The ring Sue had picked out was a very large, marquise-shaped diamond solitaire. The stone was almost as big as the fingernail on Jessica's pinky. It was set in an ornate platinum band.

"Wow," Elizabeth said. "Is that the one you like?" *Gosh,* she thought. *Such a showy diamond would look a little out of place in the rain forests of South America.*

Sue nodded decisively. "Yes. This is it. I'll have to bring Jeremy here and show it to him."

The twins met eyes over Sue's head. Elizabeth looked carefully at the ring so they could recognize it again when she came here with Jeremy.

Sue gave the ring back to the salesclerk. "Now, don't sell it to anyone else," she joked.

As the girls headed toward the parking lot, Elizabeth and Jessica let Sue wander ahead a bit so they could talk.

"Ol' Jeremy must be loaded," Jessica murmured.

"I hope so," Elizabeth whispered. "Because that ring cost almost as much as the down payment on a house."

"Maybe they won't need much money in savings, if they're just going to be traveling for a couple of years," Jessica said softly.

Elizabeth shook her head. "I don't know. It was a beautiful ring, and it looks terrific on Sue's hand. But that money could be used for so many other things."

"It sounds as if she wants a pretty elaborate wedding," Jessica added in a low voice. "I think the perfect wedding would be on the beach at sunset. Maybe barefoot or something. With family and friends, and then a wild party afterward, with a hot band."

Just then Sue skipped back to them. "You guys were so sweet to bring me here," she said. "I'm having a great time! And I just love that ring we found. You know, they say diamonds are a great investment. I always wished that I could have my mother's engagement ring, but she never really had one. I guess Daddy was too poor when they got married, and then Phil, my stepdad, never got around to giving her one." For a moment, Sue's normally cheerful face clouded over. "But that isn't going to happen to me. When Jeremy gives me my engagement ring, I want it to be nice enough to hand down to my daughter someday." She turned to give the twins a smile. "I just wish it was tomorrow night so Jeremy could be here, too. I don't know how I'm ever going to last until then!"

"We'll just have to keep you busy," Elizabeth told her, laughing. *So that explains the big ring,* Elizabeth mused. *Poor Sue. It's as if this wedding is going to give her the security she hasn't had in a long time. Not that that's the only reason she's getting married, of course. It couldn't be.*

Chapter 4

"More cold chicken, Lila?" Robby Goodman asked. They were sitting by the rippling blue water of Secca Lake on Monday afternoon.

"No, thanks. I'm stuffed." Lila lay back on the cotton blanket Robby had brought, her hands behind her head. "That was a fabulous picnic, Robby," she said dreamily. "It was a brilliant idea. You're so clever—you make everything fun."

Robby smiled down at her indulgently, his black hair falling into his eyes. "You're fun to plan things for, Lila," he said softly. "You really know how to enjoy life. I respect that."

Lila returned his smile. "So many people pretend that it's better to do without things all the time," she said, taking Robby's hand in hers. "But in a way, that's more arrogant than always going for what you want. Why turn your nose up at caviar

41

and champagne, as if beer and peanuts were just as good? Don't you agree?"

Robby stretched out close to Lila on the blanket and gently stroked a white rose against her face. "I totally agree. It's unusual for someone so young to have so much worldly wisdom," he said seriously.

Lila gave him a glowing smile. She couldn't get over the sheer happiness of the last week. Robby was one in a million, and he *had* millions too, which was a totally unbeatable combination. No other boy had ever meshed with her so perfectly, ever agreed with her so easily, ever doted on her so obviously. For the first time in her life, she had met a guy who thought she was just fine the way she was, and it felt wonderful. If only they could have met earlier. But with the age difference, and the fact that Robby had moved to Sweet Valley only two years ago, their paths had never crossed. Until now.

Looking up into his deep-blue eyes, Lila felt a thrill run down her spine. Her lips parted, and he moved nearer to her in response. Gently he kissed her, touching her waist to pull her closer to him.

They had seen each other almost every day for the last six days, and each time was better than the last. They liked the same movies, the same restaurants, the same music. Robby lived with his father, who was out of town, in a house just as beautiful and big and expensive as hers. When they had dri-

42

ven to Miller's Point in his Lamborghini, she had felt totally comfortable with him—she trusted him completely. His kisses were exciting and tempting and tender all at once. He seemed instinctively to know how far to go and when to stop. He was exactly what she wanted—and needed. Earlier in the year, Lila had almost been date-raped, and since then her love life had taken a sinking plummet. Only recently had she started to date again, but she had never felt so at ease with anyone but Robby. Maybe it was because he was older, she mused. He was twenty, by far the oldest guy she had ever dated.

"Lila, you're so beautiful," he murmured against her cheek. "So special. You're like a fine jewel—made to be cherished. I can't believe I met you." They kissed deeply again.

"I feel the same way about you," she said, looking lovingly into his eyes. "I've never met someone who's so much like me. The boys I dated before you came from different backgrounds, and they were always intimidated by my money."

Robby nodded sympathetically, then kissed her nose. She giggled.

"Do you really think our both having money is that important?" he asked. He broke into a teasing smile. "What if I were just like I am now, but broke. Would you still care?"

Lila laughed. "Robby, that's just the point. You're *not* broke. That's why you understand me so well, why we get along. We move in the same world—we like the same things. Those things happen to be the finer things in life. If you were broke, do you think you would have put together such a fabulous gourmet picnic? Would we be lying on this wonderful, soft blanket? Would we have driven here in a car that makes other people drool?" Her brown eyes shone as she gazed into his.

Thoughtfully Robby picked up a strand of her long brown hair and played with it, wrapping it around his fingers. "Lila, even if I were broke, I would somehow get those things for you. You deserve all of it, and more."

Lila's breath caught in her throat as Robby pulled her close and kissed her again. She held him tightly, never wanting to let him go. *This is it,* she thought giddily. *I'm in love.*

How repulsive, Jessica thought late that afternoon as she hung up the phone. She preferred Lila tormented and single. This bubbly, giddy, happy person was completely unnatural. She didn't know how much more of Lila's gloating she could take. "Robby's so wonderful; Robby's so fabulous. Ugh! Give me a break," Jessica muttered to herself.

A tap on her door made her look up. "Uh-huh?"

Elizabeth came in. "Jess, I— Oh, my God, what happened in here?" she asked, a horrified expression on her face.

Jessica looked at her impassively. "Very funny.

44

Maybe you could take that act on TV. You know Mom made me clean my room."

"I had no idea you had a wooden floor," Elizabeth said wonderingly, tapping it with her foot. "And you have a bed, too. I always thought you just slept on a little nest of some kind."

"You're a real laugh riot today, aren't you?" Jessica said in exasperation.

Elizabeth laughed. "Sorry. Couldn't resist. But the room looks great. It seems so much bigger and airier."

"I think it's sterile," Jessica grumbled. "I can't find anything when it's all so . . . organized."

"Excuse me, guys?" Sue poked her head in the partly open door. "Can I come in?"

"Of course," Jessica said, beckoning her in.

"What do you think of this outfit?" Sue asked nervously. "I want to look right for Jeremy." She pirouetted in front of them. She was wearing a dressy silk shorts-and-top set in a pretty shade of rose. As usual, her outfit was the latest in New York chic, but it wasn't the sort of daring look that Jessica knew *she'd* choose if she didn't have a mother around to supervise her.

"You look great," Elizabeth said. "Jeremy will definitely appreciate what he's been missing."

"You think so?" Sue looked doubtfully at her outfit. "Maybe I should wear a skirt, or dressier sandals. Or both. Bigger earrings or something."

"I think you look fine as is," Jessica said. "You

45

make me feel totally frumpy." *Well, not exactly* frumpy, she thought, looking down at her two-piece dress of black linen. There were open-work scallops all around the neck and sleeves, and the back was practically bare except for the hand embroidery.

"No, no, this outfit is all wrong," Sue said desperately. "I have to go change." Turning, she fled down the hall to Steven's room.

The twins looked at each other and smiled. "I know how she feels," Jessica said. "If I were about to meet the love of my life again, I think I would be throwing up in the bathroom."

Elizabeth chuckled. "I just wanted to tell you that I think you've been great with Sue the last few days. I know your mystery man is still on your mind, but you've really put yourself out to help Sue and make her feel welcome, and I'm proud of you." She reached over and gave Jessica a spontaneous hug.

Jessica hugged her back and sighed. "I like Sue a lot, but it's been really hard, listening to her go on about how much in love she is, and how perfect ol' Jeremy is. I feel as though I've known him my whole life, the way she talks about him constantly."

"Saint Jeremy," Elizabeth giggled.

"Jeremy the Wise," Jessica said with a smirk.

"Jeremy the Beneficent." Elizabeth started laughing out loud.

"What's worse is that even loser-at-love Lila has someone. I feel like I'm in the middle of a conspiracy. I have to watch everyone else be happy while I'm alone and miserable." Jessica grimaced, then headed into the bathroom that connected the girls' two bedrooms. She fumbled around in her makeup drawer and started fixing her face.

Elizabeth followed her. "Why mess with perfection?" she teased as Jessica carefully brushed a bit of blush across her high cheekbones.

"I just want to present a good face. There's no reason why the whole world has to know my heart is broken into a thousand pieces."

"Well, that's a switch," Elizabeth said. "Since when are you such a private-type person?"

"I *mean*, I don't have to look like a hag just because I'm destined to be single all my life," Jessica continued. Her hand was steady as she outlined her eyes with a smoky gray eyeliner pencil.

"Do you still really care about him so much? You were only with him five minutes, almost a week ago."

Jessica stopped and looked into Elizabeth's eyes. "Yeah. I still care about him. When he ran off like that, it was as if someone had taken the actual air out of my lungs." She sighed and turned back to the mirror to give her hair a good brushing.

"Should I wear it up or down?" she asked Elizabeth, looking at herself critically.

"Up always looks elegant." Elizabeth stood beside her and drew her own hair back with matching faux tortoiseshell combs. Catching Jessica's glance in the mirror, she said, "Do you think I'm a complete dope when it comes to relationships?" Her blue-green eyes suddenly looked haunted.

"No more than any other sixteen-year-old," Jessica said airily. Then, seeing Elizabeth's real distress, she said, "Liz, so you made a mistake with Luke. Big deal. People do it all the time. Just concentrate on Todd and forget it ever happened." She patted Elizabeth's shoulder briskly.

"Not people, Jessica. Women."

"What? What are you talking about?"

"People don't make mistakes all the time. Women do. Women constantly make mistakes about men. And I'm no exception. That's why it's so important for me to really understand myself and my motivations. My book is really helping me. But the more I read, the more issues I feel I have to work on. Boyfriends, myself, my self-esteem. I keep getting pulled in different directions. I've started reading another book, too."

"Good, good," Jessica murmured, pushing in the last hairpin. Her hair was now coiled loosely on top her head in a soft, romantic bun. "How do I look?"

"Gorgeous. It's called *Primal Woman, Woman of Strength.*"

Jessica frowned at her. "What is?"

"The new book I'm reading."

Jessica lightly spritzed her hair with a bit of holding spray. "Elizabeth—maybe you're going overboard with this self-help stuff. I mean, why don't you just hang out and not worry about it so much?"

Elizabeth sighed and surveyed her summery, yellow sleeveless jumpsuit with wide, flowing legs in the mirror. "I just need a little guidance to steer clear of romantic pitfalls. Anyway, I guess I'll go see if Mom needs any help in the kitchen."

"I'll be down in a minute." Jessica grinned. "As soon as you've finished helping her and there's nothing left for me to do."

Elizabeth laughed. "You'll never change." She left through her bedroom and headed downstairs.

There, Jessica thought, putting the finishing touches on her makeup. But somehow the sight of her perfectly primped face only made her realize how horrible she really felt. Heading back to her room, she wanted to flop down on her neatly made bed and burst into tears. How could she go on living, knowing that she would never see her dream man again, never feel his kiss? Never would she plan her own wedding, never would she have blond, dark-eyed children. Jessica bit back a sob, determined not to ruin her makeup. She would just have to muddle through the rest of her life one day, one hour, one minute at a time.

Sighing heavily, Jessica left her room and headed downstairs. There was no point in avoiding it. Soon she would have to meet Sue's Mr. Perfect, and she would have to smile and be polite and make conversation with someone she could care less about. He was probably chunky, she decided, plodding down the stairs. Maybe he was already losing his hair.

The front doorbell rang when she was halfway down the stairs.

"Jess, could you get that?" her mother called from the dining room.

"OK," she called back. She unthinkingly patted her hair into place as she opened the door.

"Hi, you must be—" Jessica froze in midsentence, her eyes wide. She was dreaming. She must still be upstairs in her room, sound asleep on her bed, wrinkling the dress that had taken all afternoon to iron.

There, standing on the front porch, was the gorgeous stranger, *her* gorgeous stranger, looking at her with as much shock as she felt.

Jessica's heart leapt and her face broke into a radiant smile. He had come back for her. He had found her somehow. They would actually be together. She would get married and have children, after all.

"You're here," she breathed, drinking him in hungrily with her eyes. He was as tall as she remembered, with wide, powerful shoulders and slim hips. His honey-blond hair was trimmed slightly, still curling in unruly waves around his neck. As attractive as he had been in his black swim trunks, he looked even more handsome in his khaki pants, white shirt, and navy jacket. His shirt was open at the throat, and Jessica's eyes fastened on the beating of his pulse there.

As if in a dream, she took a step closer toward him. Unbidden, her arms began to lift, soon to circle around his neck. He stood stiffly, with a panicked look on his face. Jessica saw the longing in his eyes. He wanted her; she could feel it.

"Jeremy!" A happy shriek in back of Jessica made her jump. She turned to look at Sue as she ran down the stairs and toward the front door, toward Jessica's true love. Jessica stared uncomprehendingly as Sue brushed past her and threw her arms around the beautiful stranger. Jessica's mouth dropped open as the stranger's arms came up to circle Sue's back.

"Jeremy, Jeremy," Sue was murmuring into his tanned neck. "I missed you so much. I can't believe you're finally here." Her eyes shining, she lifted her face to his. Jessica watched as Jeremy, Sue's wonderful fiancé and the one true love of Jessica's life, bent his head and kissed Sue on the lips. His coal-dark eyes burned into Jessica's for an instant before closing shut.

Chapter 5

Pulling away after their kiss, Sue turned a glowing face to Jessica. "Jessica, I'd like you to meet my fiancé, Jeremy Randall." She gave a tinkling laugh. "I've talked about him so much, you probably feel like you know him already."

"Yes, I do," Jessica said in a low voice. Her face was burning, her heart heavy.

Jessica's dream man stepped forward and held out his hand. "How do you do, Jessica?" he said huskily, not meeting her eyes.

You know very well how I do, Jessica thought numbly. *This can't be happening. This is a nightmare. This is much worse than never seeing you again.* With every ounce of willpower she possessed, she forced herself to hold out her own suddenly icy hand, and let it be enveloped by his strong brown one. *But you're mine,* her mind protested futilely. *You know you're mine.*

Then Elizabeth and Mrs. Wakefield were behind her, and they were all smiling and shaking hands. When Jeremy first saw Elizabeth, he started visibly, looking quickly from her back to Jessica. Then he gave a small nod and smiled casually.

"I'm so pleased to meet you," Elizabeth said. "According to Sue, you're perfect in every way."

"He is!" Sue protested.

Jeremy's warm laughter filled the foyer.

"Jeremy, welcome," Mrs. Wakefield said. "If there's anything we can help you with while you're here, please let us know."

"Thank you."

"Now come in. You must be hungry after that long flight," Mrs. Wakefield said chattily. "We have some appetizers set up in the family room. Was your plane on time?"

"Excuse me," Jessica said and quickly shut herself up in the first-floor powder room as her mother led the others down the hall. She leaned trembling against the sink, feeling as if she was going to be sick. The only man she would ever love was engaged to marry another woman. And that woman was Sue Gibbons. And that was why he'd said he couldn't ever see her again.

Jessica sat down on the closed toilet lid for a minute, a cool washcloth against her forehead.

She remembered Sue telling her that he was twenty-three—he was older than she had thought. But his kiss had been so sincere—their connection so obvious. What she had seen in his eyes at the beach that day had been real, had been lasting. . . .

Get a grip, she told herself. If he could be so cool and collected, so could she. *Sure you're totally, irrevocably, dangerously in love with him, but that doesn't mean you have no pride.* After splashing water on her face, she walked calmly out to the family room, where her parents, Elizabeth, and Sue were all talking and laughing with Jeremy.

"And you've met Jessica," Alice Wakefield said cheerfully as Jessica entered the room.

Jeremy met her eyes for a split second. "Yes, briefly," he said with a smile.

Jessica smiled at him noncommittally and took her place beside Elizabeth on the couch. She was rewarded by the slightest hint of his lips tightening. *Jeremy,* she thought, keeping her expression blank. Now she knew his name at last. *Jeremy. Jeremy and Jessica. J and J. Jessica Randall.* As she watched him holding hands with Sue, talking and laughing with Elizabeth and their parents, her heart constricted painfully. At least Elizabeth had no idea this was the same man Jessica had been mooning over for the past week. Right now Jessica had no patience for one of Elizabeth's "be sensible" lectures.

As though in a dream, Jessica got up with the others when it was time for dinner. Mr. Wakefield had prepared one of Jessica's favorite meals: his famous oven-fried chicken, mashed potatoes, and sugar snap peas. But tonight she could hardly taste anything. She was sitting next to Elizabeth and across from Jeremy and Sue at the dining room table. With every bite that she forced down, she felt Jeremy's dark eyes on her, watching her. She refused to look at him—she had never felt so betrayed in her life. He had chosen to marry someone else. *But has he really chosen? Obviously he has, Jessica,* she told herself. *Nobody forced him to ask Sue to be his wife.*

"Jessica?"

Looking up quickly, she saw that Sue was smiling at her from across the table.

Jessica smiled back. Fortunately, she'd had a lot of practice hiding her feelings. "I'm sorry—what did you say?"

"I said, tell Jeremy all the places you and Elizabeth have taken me in the last three days. I can't remember half of them." She turned an excited face to her fiancé. "They've been so sweet to me, Jeremy. I've had the best time. I'm almost ready to move to Sweet Valley for good! Do you think we could live here, with our jobs and everything?"

56

Jessica's heart contracted as Jeremy smiled down at Sue. "I don't know, sweetie. We've carved out a niche for ourselves in New York. But we'll talk about it, OK?" He reached across and casually rubbed Sue's back. She beamed and leaned against him, like a kitten preening under his touch. Jessica concentrated on sipping her water so she wouldn't have to look at them. *If they move here, I'm taking off for Alaska.*

"Let's see—we went to the Beach Cafe, we played tennis at the country club, we went shopping. . . ." Elizabeth started ticking off their activities on her fingers.

"We went to the mall, and to the Dairi Burger—hmmm, and what else? We went to the *beach.* . . ." Jessica said deliberately, meeting Jeremy's eyes. He looked straight back at her calmly. *Why are you pretending that our kiss never happened?*

"Wow! I hope you girls haven't been running Sue ragged. She's going to need her strength for the next few weeks," Mrs. Wakefield joked. "Speaking of which, have you two decided what kind of wedding you'd like?"

"We haven't really talked about it," Sue said, gazing adoringly into Jeremy's eyes.

"Since it's going to be here in Sweet Valley, it makes sense to utilize the natural beauty of the area," Jeremy said in his slightly husky voice that sent chills down Jessica's spine. "On the flight

57

over here, I was thinking that maybe we could have a nice, simple ceremony on the beach, with just some friends and our families. Something small, but special." He looked at Sue expectantly.

Elizabeth laughed. "That's funny. We were talking about weddings the other day, and that's exactly the kind of wedding Jessica said she wanted." Elizabeth looked at her sister fondly. "She said maybe she'd even go barefoot—and then have a wild party afterward, with a band." Everyone around the table laughed—everyone except Jeremy.

Jessica smiled tightly and looked down at the pattern she was making in her mashed potatoes. *See,* she telegraphed to Jeremy. *You said we hardly knew each other, but this is proof that we're meant to be together, the two halves of the same person.*

"Well, I don't know if I'll go barefoot, but if Jeremy wants to be married on a beach, it sounds fine to me. As long as we're together," Sue said.

What about your big fancy church wedding? Jessica wondered.

"What are your plans for tomorrow?" Mrs. Wakefield asked Sue and Jeremy. For the last half-hour they had been drinking coffee out on the patio and talking about the young couple's wedding plans.

Looking over at Elizabeth, Sue said, "Elizabeth has offered to take me to the bookstore tomorrow to buy a wedding planner."

"That's a good idea. It'll help us keep track of all the details," Mrs. Wakefield agreed.

"Then," Elizabeth said, smiling, "Jessica and I have to get together with Jeremy for a while."

Jeremy raised his eyebrows. "Oh?"

"Yes," Elizabeth said. "Mom, maybe you could show Sue your office tomorrow afternoon. I'm sure you'll have some great ideas about the kinds of decorations we can use on the beach." Mrs. Wakefield had her own interior decorating firm in downtown Sweet Valley.

"That would be great," Sue said.

"I'd be happy to," Mrs. Wakefield agreed. She sat back in her chair and gazed up at the sky. "Look at that beautiful moon. I hope we have such perfect weather for your wedding."

"We will," Sue said firmly. "Sweetie, I have a great idea. Why don't we take your car and drive to the beach now?" she suggested to Jeremy. "I think I can find the way there by myself. Wouldn't the beach be pretty at night?"

"Uh-oh. I think the young lovebirds want some time alone," Ned Wakefield teased. "The beach is a very romantic place at night."

Sue blushed becomingly. "Can we?" she asked Jeremy again.

Half hidden in the shadows of their small palm

tree, Jessica watched Jeremy's face intently. Indecision played across his handsome features, but at Sue's beseeching look, he smiled and agreed.

"You have a rental car, don't you?" Mrs. Wakefield asked.

"Yes. It's right out front," Jeremy responded.

"The way to the beach is really easy," Elizabeth confirmed. "But if you guys get lost or anything, just call us and we'll come rescue you."

Sue and Jeremy laughed. His laughter sent a thrill through Jessica's spine.

"It's a deal," he said. He stood up and shook Mr. and Mrs. Wakefield's hands. "Thank you for a wonderful dinner," he said. He looked over at Elizabeth. "Nice meeting you. I'll see you tomorrow." Then Jeremy sought out Jessica's face in the deepening shadows. His eyes met hers, and she sat very still. "Nice meeting you," he said. She nodded quickly and looked away, biting her lip.

Mrs. Wakefield led them back through the house, making sure that Sue had a key to let herself back in.

For a moment Jessica sat in her lawn chair, torturing herself with images of Sue and Jeremy in his car. She imagined the beach, moonlight glowing on the white sand, the cool ocean breeze, the feeling of privacy and magic. The long kisses, the murmured sighs, the happiness the couple felt at being back together . . .

60

But Sue isn't the one for him. His laughter, his wish for a beach wedding, echoed through Jessica's mind. More than ever, Jessica knew that Jeremy was the one for her. Even as she also knew that she would definitely never have him.

Chapter 6

"Since you guys made dinner, we'll clean up," Elizabeth told her parents. "Right, Jess?"

"OK," Jessica said.

"Thanks, honey." Her mother came over and kissed Elizabeth good night, then hugged Jessica, too. "Good night, sweetheart."

"Night, Mom." Jessica absently began to stack coffee cups on their tray.

"Jess?"

Elizabeth was standing next to her, a look of concern on her face.

"What?"

"All through dinner you looked as if you had just eaten a jellyfish. What's wrong?"

"Nothing," Jessica lied. She gave her sister a bright smile. "Why?"

Narrowing her eyes, Elizabeth stared at Jessica.

"Look, I've known you for sixteen years. You can't fool me. Why were you so quiet tonight? Are you still upset over your mystery man? Did seeing Sue and Jeremy so happy make it harder for you?"

Jessica looked into her twin's face, so like her own. The gentle, caring concern she saw there broke something deep inside her. No matter what, Elizabeth was always there for her. Dropping her tray with a clatter, Jessica threw her arms around Elizabeth and burst into tears.

"Oh, Liz! You won't believe it. It's so horrible," she sobbed.

Elizabeth patted Jessica's back. "What is it? Please tell me, Jess. Maybe I can help."

Jessica cried against Elizabeth's shoulder for a few more minutes, releasing the pent-up emotion that had been seething all night. Hiccuping, Jessica stepped back and wiped her eyes with her hands. "Liz—I don't know what to do. Remember my mysterious stranger? The one I knew I was destined to be with?"

"How could I not remember? I've heard about him every day for the last week," Elizabeth teased gently. She led Jessica into the brightly lit kitchen and wet a paper towel under the tap. Then she carefully stroked it around Jessica's eyes, removing the smeared mascara. "Now sit down and tell me what's going on," she said firmly.

They sat at the butcher-block kitchen table, and Jessica wrung the paper towel in her nervous fingers. "It's Jeremy," Jessica finally whispered in a broken voice.

Elizabeth looked perplexed. "What's Jeremy? What about him?"

Turning anguished eyes to her sister, Jessica repeated, "My fantasy guy. The one who kissed me on the beach. It was Jeremy."

Elizabeth stared at Jessica. She must not have heard right. This would be too big a mess for even Jessica to have gotten herself into. "What? How could it have been? He just flew in from New York this afternoon."

"He was here last week on business. He must have been arranging for him and Sue to work in Los Angeles while they're here planning the wedding. He was the one at the beach that day, Liz. He was playing Frisbee with his friend, the one who's dating Lila now. I met him, and he kissed me, and we knew we were supposed to be together. Then he said we couldn't see each other anymore and ran off. Now I know why." Jessica started to weep into her paper towel.

"Jess," Elizabeth began carefully, her mind whirring, "this is just incredible. I mean, he's engaged to be married. And he's so much older."

"I know," Jessica said, straightening up and drying her eyes. "But it's a mistake. He knows it and I know it."

"But Sue doesn't know it," Elizabeth reminded her. "Jess, you wouldn't—I mean, they're planning on getting married. You wouldn't—"

"Ruin their wedding? Make a scene? Give me a little credit, Liz. I can see that Jeremy's made his choice. I'm not going to embarrass myself by running after someone who's obviously chosen the wrong woman."

Elizabeth touched her sister's hand. "Maybe Jeremy, on the beach—maybe he was just sowing his last wild oat," she said gently. "He knew he was about to get married forever, and he saw a really pretty girl, and something clicked, and it just happened." Elizabeth walked to the freezer. "Fudge ripple or coffee Heath-bar crunch?"

"Coffee."

Elizabeth dished up two bowls of ice cream and handed one to Jessica. "You know, I was really starting to like Jeremy."

"What's not to like?" Jessica snuffled, taking a small bite of her medicinal ice cream.

"Well, the fact that he was kissing pretty girls on the beach while his fiancée was three thousand miles away sort of makes me think he's got a few kinks to straighten out," Elizabeth replied.

"He was kissing *me*, singular, not girls, plural."

"Whatever. He was already committed somewhere else." Elizabeth licked her spoon thoughtfully, looking through the sliding glass doors out into the night. "It just goes to show you how troubled the relationships between men and women are. If Sue were really strong within herself, maybe Jeremy wouldn't be attracted to other women."

66

"Woman," Jessica corrected.

"And if you were really strong within yourself," Elizabeth continued as though she hadn't heard Jessica, "you wouldn't be attracted to men who aren't available. My book *Real Women, Bad Men* says that having a pattern of being attracted to men who are taken is a sign of—"

"Like your being attracted to Bruce Patman?" Jessica pointed out impatiently. "When he was already going out with Pamela Robertson." Bruce Patman was a year older than they were, but they had known him almost his whole life. He was a spoiled, filthy-rich, snobby guy, but that hadn't stopped either of them from getting involved with him. Elizabeth's aborted romance with Bruce hadn't been that long ago. It had almost broken her and Todd up, and caused major problems for Bruce and Pamela.

Elizabeth winced. "Low blow. We were just trying to get his parents back together."

"His parents weren't the only people you got together. Everyone saw you two kissing in the kitchen that night."

"OK. OK. I never said I didn't need to do more soul-searching, Jess. I know I need to get myself together. That's why I've been reading these self-help books in the first place. I'm only saying—"

"Yeah, yeah. I need to be stronger within myself, as a woman," Jessica said tiredly.

"Exactly!" Elizabeth beamed at her.

Jessica sighed. Elizabeth didn't usually miss the point, but when she did, she missed it by at least a mile.

Please help me feel a tiny bit human, that's all I ask of you, Jessica silently begged her shower, first hot, then cold, on Tuesday morning.

Her skin began to wrinkle under the water, but she still felt disoriented by her dreams from the night before—Sam, kissing her on a beach, then saying he couldn't see her anymore; Elizabeth marching in a picket line, carrying a sign that said "Strong Women Unite"; Sue in a wedding dress, looking radiant. And then Jessica and Jeremy, kissing each other deeply in a white convertible with "Just Married" written on it in shaving cream.

As she stared at herself in the foggy bathroom mirror, she remembered something that snapped her completely awake. *I'm seeing Jeremy today.* She and Elizabeth had made plans to take him to the Valley Mall to get Sue's engagement ring. *You're a total idiot,* Jessica told herself as she untangled her wet hair. *Do you think a strong woman would actually go with her soul mate to the mall to buy a ring for someone else?* Flinging down the brush in disgust, she stomped back into her room to get dressed.

Ten minutes later she was in the kitchen in a summery white halter dress with a full, softly draped skirt and white espadrilles. She wore her blond hair in a pretty French braid. The kitchen was quiet—her parents were already at work. After taking a container of yogurt from the fridge, she sat at the table where she had cried in front of Elizabeth the night before.

As she spooned the first bite into her mouth, she saw the note propped against the saltshaker.

> Jess—
>
> I'm taking Sue to the Fern Street Bookshop to get a wedding planner. I'll drop her at Mom's office at 11:30, then come get you by twelve. If Jeremy calls, tell him we'll pick him up at 12:30. We'll have lunch before going to the mall.
>
> See you—
> E.

The bottom of the note was folded up, and Jessica smoothed it with her hand. In a hastily scribbled P.S., Elizabeth had written, "No funny business. This means *you*."

Jessica laughed out loud. *Whatever would make you think there'd be any funny business, Liz?* She glanced at the clock above the stove. It was ten thirty. There must be some way she could turn this situation to her advantage.

When the phone rang a few minutes later, Jessica had a vague plan perking in her brain. "Hello?"

"Hello—is this Elizabeth?"

Jessica drew in a sharp breath. She would know his sexy, slightly husky voice anywhere.

"No," she said coolly.

There was a moment of silence. Then, "Jessica? This is Jeremy."

"I know."

"Oh. Well, last night Elizabeth said something about getting together today. Do you know what it's about?"

"Yes. Sue showed us a ring she likes at the jewelry store at the mall. We wanted to take you there so you could buy it and . . . surprise Sue."

Pause. "That's a great idea. Should I come over there?"

Jessica knew exactly what she wanted to do. "Yes, could you? Elizabeth left me a note saying she would meet us at the mall at eleven thirty. If you come pick me up, I'll give you directions."

Another long silence. *Come on, just do it.*

"OK. I'll see you in a few minutes."

Jessica hung up the phone, then jumped in the air. *Yes!* She punched the air. In just a few minutes she would be with her true love again. They would be alone in a car. It would be heaven, sheer heaven. Except for the tiny detail that he was getting married to the Wakefields' houseguest in a little over three weeks.

"So, how did you and Sue meet?" Jessica asked casually, leaning her arm against the window of

70

Jeremy's white rental car. *No reason to let him know I already know.* They were on their way to the Valley Mall, and it was another typically beautiful California morning. Fortunately for Jessica, they had managed to leave the house before Elizabeth came back.

"It was at Project Nature. I've worked there since I finished college, and Sue began a while ago as an intern."

"Take a left here," Jessica broke in.

"OK. Sue was assigned to help on a project I was conducting, so we were thrown together a lot. I think we both admired the other's commitment to our work. Gradually we began liking each other, then we were really fond of each other, then it just sort of seemed to make sense for us to get married, so we could continue to work together no matter where we are."

Jessica looked out the window, her heart beating fast. *Jeremy's version of their meeting sure sounded different from his fiancée's. What happened to the sparks-flying, love-at-first-sight business that Sue had described on the beach a few days ago?* Smiling secretly to herself, Jessica wondered how he would have described *their* meeting. As Jeremy drove expertly down the main road leading to the mall, Jessica remembered an old saying that her French friend Rene had told her in London, just a few weeks ago. Translated, it meant something like, "In every relationship there is the

71

one who kisses, and the one who is kissed." It was clear to Jessica, if not to Jeremy, that Sue was the one doing the kissing in this relationship.

"There's the mall entrance," Jessica said, pointing. "So I guess you can park anywhere around here."

"OK," Jeremy said. His long tan fingers steered the rental car into a spot, then he cut the engine. He took the keys out of the ignition, but made no move to get out. Jessica looked calmly out her window, refusing to meet his gaze.

"Jessica— I . . . think we need to talk about what happened last week on the beach."

Jessica turned and gave him a bright, careless smile. "Oh, don't worry. I never even had a bruise. You might want to work on your Frisbee catch, though. Shall we go?" She opened her door and swished out.

Inside the mall, Jessica led Jeremy toward Bibi's. "This is just about the nicest jewelry store in Sweet Valley," she said, guiding him inside. "We had fun looking at rings with Sue."

Jeremy nodded and followed her into the store. "Wait—don't tell me which one she picked out. Let me see if I can find it myself. It's more romantic that way."

Jessica's eyes narrowed slightly as he gave her a sardonic, meaningful smile. *So, you're playing "two can play at that game," eh? Well, you better watch out, Jeremy. You're playing with fire, and you're going to get burned.*

Jeremy walked slowly around the store, looking into each glass case. Finally he looked up and motioned Jessica over. "I think I've found it," he told her.

She raised her eyebrows.

Triumphantly, he leaned over a case and tapped his finger on the glass. "That one. Second from the top."

Jessica leaned over the glass, her French braid brushing against her bare back. She had to control her gasp. The ring he had chosen was an oval blue sapphire, with a small triangular diamond on each side. Her ring, the one she had picked out. *It's the ring we're meant to share.*

"No, Jeremy," she said, forcing a bored tone. "Actually, that's the ring I chose. Sue's favorite ring is over here." She walked in brisk, businesslike steps over to the next case and searched for the large diamond solitaire that Sue had liked. "Here it is."

A salesclerk bustled over and opened the case. "A beautiful ring," she cooed, taking the marquise-shaped diamond ring out of its box. "And it will look so beautiful on your charming fiancée."

Before they realized what was happening, the salesclerk lifted Jessica's left hand and slid the ring onto her third finger. "Why don't you two admire it for a moment? Take your time, and call if you need me."

Jessica stared down at the large ring on her finger. She tilted her hand, and the diamond flashed with sparkly lights. Beautiful, of course—but so large on her slim finger. *The glare off this thing would give me a headache,* she thought, and looked up to find Jeremy gazing at her with heated intensity.

He took her hand with his and held it loosely, as though to examine the ring. Just the touch of his hand on hers made Jessica's cheeks flush. If only . . .

"Well, this is the one Sue liked," Jessica said shortly, sliding the ring off her finger and dropping it into Jeremy's palm. *If only we were here to buy our engagement ring,* she thought sadly.

"Are you sure this is the one Sue liked?" he asked, looking doubtfully at the ring.

"Yep."

"Well, OK, I guess." Jeremy called the sales-clerk over and paid for the ring, widening his eyes a little at the price.

"Would you two like to see the matching wedding band now?" the salesclerk said. "I'm sure your lovely young fiancée would like to see them together." She smiled at Jessica.

"No," Jeremy said firmly. "No, thank you." Taking Jessica by the elbow, he steered her out the store and into the mall.

"It was a natural mistake for her to make," he said, once they were walking along the mall corridor back to the car.

"Oh, sure," Jessica said, pretending to look at a new bathing suit in the window at Lisette's. "No prob."

Jeremy paused to stand beside her in front of

the window, and Jessica's heart plummeted when she saw their reflections there. They looked so perfect together, so right. Two blond heads, his darker, hers lighter . . .

"Yo. Wakefield."

Whirling, Jessica found herself facing Bruce Patman's mocking smile. "Doing a little shopping?" he asked sarcastically. "How unusual."

"Take a hike, Bruce," she said automatically, not bothering to introduce him to Jeremy. Bruce smirked and walked on, taking another big bite of his soft pretzel.

"Friend of yours?" Jeremy asked.

"Only if you use the broadest definition of friend," Jessica replied, heading for the mall doors. Bruce Patman was good-looking and sexy and rich, three of her favorite qualities, but he was also a pompous jerk. They'd been best enemies ever since they'd dated for a very brief, disastrous time, calling a temporary truce only to put her parents' marriage back together.

"Jessica, wait."

"What, Jeremy?" When she heard his gorgeous voice speak her name, her heart skipped. She looked into his beautiful eyes. Was this the moment of truth?

"What about Elizabeth? Weren't we supposed to meet her here?"

Jessica turned back to the doors. *He's thinking of* Elizabeth? *Oh, what's the use?* "I lied, Jeremy.

Elizabeth was supposed to meet me back at the house, then we were going to pick you up."

Pushing through the doors after her, Jeremy took her arm, forcing her to look up at him. She stared defiantly into his deep, dark eyes.

"You lied? Why?"

"So I could be with you alone, of course." Jessica made a wry grimace and shook her arm loose. "Isn't that pathetic?"

Chapter 7

In a way, this is my own darn fault, Elizabeth thought as she waited on Jessica's bed for her up-to-no-good sister to come home. Leaving Jessica here with that note was like leaving a jar of honey next to an anthill.

Jeremy was probably tied up and gagged in the trunk of his car by now, as Jessica drove them fast toward the Mexican border, Elizabeth thought. It would be funny if it weren't so serious.

"I know, I know, I'm a terrible person," Jessica said irritably, when she finally came home and found her sister in her room. "I just had to be with him, Liz. I can't explain it."

"I can. It's spelled S-E-L-F-I-S-H."

Jessica grimaced at her and dropped her purse on the dresser. "So, did you have a good time at the bookstore with Sue this morning?" she asked breezily.

"Uh-huh. Sue was getting all worked up about which wedding planner to buy. I was looking through a couple of biographies I've been wanting to read. Jess, I'm almost afraid to ask, but did you and Jeremy go get Sue's ring this morning?"

"Yes, as a matter of fact, we did."

Elizabeth sighed and looked up at the ceiling of Jessica's room. "And *which* ring did you tell him to get, Jess? Take your time, and think about what you want to tell me."

Jessica stalked over to Elizabeth and put her hands on her hips. "Elizabeth Wakefield, what do you think I am? For your information, Jeremy wanted to guess which ring Sue had picked out, and then—what do you know—he immediately went for the one *I* chose. But did I let him buy it? Noooo. I didn't. I swallowed my pride and pushed him in the direction of that enormous, gaudy rock Sue wanted. And he bought it! So there."

Jessica flounced into the bathroom. Elizabeth followed her and stood in the doorway as her sister splashed water on her face. "I'm sorry, Jess. But I'm worried about you. This situation could really explode, and I don't want you getting hurt." Her face lit up. "I have an idea. Why don't you come with me to Enid's house this afternoon? A bunch of us are getting together for dinner, and we're each bringing a self-help book. Then we're going to sit around and give one another personality quizzes—you know, really try to dig deep and find out what makes us tick."

Jessica dried her face with a towel. "Forgive me if I don't jump up and down at the thought." She headed back into her room.

"Come on, Jess, it'll be fun. We're going to have a cookout and talk about guys, and really try to bare our innermost feelings."

A knock on Jessica's door interrupted them, and Sue poked her head in. "Hi! Your mom just dropped me off. Can I come in?"

"Of course," Jessica said.

"I was just telling Jessica about my plans for the evening," Elizabeth explained. "Some of my friends and I are going to get together for a girls-only evening to explore our relationships—not only with one another, but with our boyfriends, too." Elizabeth paused. "I'm trying to come to terms with a bad experience I had in England."

"That's too bad," Sue said sympathetically. "I don't know you that well, Elizabeth, but from what I've seen, you seem to have good relationships with the people around you. And you're kind, considerate, loyal—I mean, no matter what you're feeling about yourself now, I still think you're a pretty terrific person."

Elizabeth was touched. "Thanks, Sue. That makes me feel better. I've been realizing that one way of combating my feelings of self-doubt is to strengthen my bonds with other women—really take solace in sisterhood, you know? So your support means a lot to me."

"Women have to stick together, that's for sure," Sue said, sitting down at Jessica's desk. Elizabeth looked at her sister. *Hear that Jess? No funny business behind Sue's back.*

"Listen, why don't you come tonight—both of you? We'll be talking about getting to know ourselves better. And the more each person knows herself, the better her relationships will be."

"It sounds really interesting, Elizabeth, but I'm afraid that Jeremy and I already have plans. We're going out to dinner at the Carousel, just the two of us. Your mom said it was a romantic restaurant." Her face glowed. "Jeremy said it was important that we be alone tonight."

"The Carousel?" Jessica asked, her voice trembling a little.

Elizabeth shot her a look. The Carousel was one of Jessica's favorite restaurants. It obviously hurt her to think of Jeremy going there with someone else. *Wait a minute—what am I thinking? Jeremy and Jessica have never even gone out! They have no "couple" memories of any place in Sweet Valley. Except, maybe, a few square feet of beach.* Elizabeth sighed. Even she was getting caught up in Jessica's unrealistic fantasies!

"That sounds really wonderful, Sue," she said enthusiastically. "I know you'll have a good time. Have you guys been talking about the wedding a lot?"

"Yes, but there's so much to do. Right now I'm

going to go to my room and go through my new wedding planner. I have to decide exactly how formal the wedding will be, and if it will be religious or not, and how we want the beach set up." She laughed, rolling her eyes. "I'm really worried I'll never get it done in time."

"Don't worry," Elizabeth said reassuringly. "You've got us, and Mom, to help you. I'm sure we'll get everything together, just the way you and Jeremy want it."

"Thanks, Elizabeth," Sue said warmly, standing up to go to Steven's room. "And you too, Jessica. I don't know what I'd do without you." She beamed at both girls before leaving the room.

"Well, I've got to get going too," Elizabeth said. "I guess it'll be just you and the 'rents for dinner. Are you sure you don't want to come?"

"No, thanks. I think it'd be better if I do all my introspecting by myself."

"OK. I'll see you later, then. And *be good*," she added meaningfully, going through the bathroom toward her own room.

"You know the old saying," Jessica said very softly. "If I can't be good, I'll be careful."

"Aaron? Jessica. Hi! What? Oh, nothing. I was just wondering if you wanted to go out to dinner with me. Tonight. No reason. No, why do you say that? Aaron! Aaron? Hello?"

❖   ❖   ❖

"A.J.? Jessica. Hi, what's up? Long time no talk. Are you busy tonight? I was thinking maybe dinner. Maybe the Carousel. Of course not. Why would I have an ulterior motive? That really hurts me, A.J. I mean, that really— A.J.? A.J.!"

"Winston? Jessica. What are you doing tonight? Oh. Do you think Maria would want to go see it another night? Oh. All week, huh? That's too bad. Oh, no reason. I better run. Enjoy the movie—tell Maria hi."

"Patman residence."

"Bruce, is that you? It's Jessica."

"To what do I owe the honor of this call, Wakefield? Are you finally going to offer to pay for the scratch you put on my car?"

"Earth to Bruce. I didn't put any scratch on your car. Listen, I'm calling because I need a tiny favor. A friend of mine has a blind date tonight, and she's asked me to show up at the same restaurant to keep an eye on her in case he's weird or something. But I can't go by myself. That would look too . . . obvious and . . ."

His rumbling laugh interrupted her. "Wakefield, you're too much. This is crazy, even for you. Now tell me the real story."

"That *was* the real story, Bruce!" Jessica said indignantly. "Why would I make something like that up? Now please, will you do me this one favor? I mean, after all I did to help get your parents back together . . ." she wheedled.

"You mean besides getting stuck in the elevator, sending my mom the wrong cassette tape, giving her an allergic reaction that sent her to the hospital, being late for—"

"OK, OK," Jessica snapped. "So there were a few snags. But I did expend a great deal of effort and energy on plans to help you. It's not my fault they took a while to work. Your folks are back together, aren't they?"

"Well, yeah . . ."

"And I helped do it, didn't I?"

"I guess, in a way . . ."

"Then take me to dinner tonight at the Carousel."

"What am I supposed to tell Pamela? The whole thing with Elizabeth nearly broke us up for good. I don't want to lose her. She's the only sane girl I've ever dated."

Jessica gritted her teeth and counted to twenty by fives. Obviously Bruce was lumping her into the "insane girlfriend" category.

"Tell her the truth," Jessica said finally. "That I've asked you to do this as a personal favor. Tell her you can't stand me, and I can't stand you. Tell her she can trust me because I'd rather have poison ivy than ever date you again!"

"OK. That's what I'll tell her. But you're going to owe me one. And you're paying for dinner. What time should I come get you?"

"Oh, thank you, Bruce, thank you. I'll make it up to you. I promise."

"I doubt it, but I'll try to think of how you can repay me. Now, what time?"

"What do you feel like doing for dinner tonight, sweetie?" Lila asked Robby. They were lying by the pool at Fowler Crest, Lila's huge, Spanish-style estate in the hills of Sweet Valley. That morning they had played tennis at Robby's house, then had lunch at Lila's house. They had been lazily basking in the sun ever since.

Robby put down his museum catalogue. "Hmmm. I don't know. How about some roast Lila with barbecue sauce?" Leaning over, he took a playful nip at her slender ankle, right above the gold ankle chain he had given her.

Yelping, Lila pulled her foot away, then swatted his arm. "You weirdo." She laughed.

"Yes, but I'm *your* weirdo," Robby said, kissing her on the mouth.

Lila eagerly kissed him back. She could kiss him endlessly, for the rest of her life. "Hmmm, true," she murmured. "And I'm glad." Sitting back against her lounge chair, she noticed the book in his lap. "Have you been reading while I was asleep? What book is that?"

"It's a catalogue of a recent art show at the Whitney Museum in New York," Robby explained.

"They put on a show recently by one of my favorite modern artists."

"Like that fabulous art you showed me at the museum yesterday?" When Robby took her to the Sweet Valley art museum the day before, Lila felt that she was really appreciating art for the first time. Robby was so knowledgeable, showing her that the paintings weren't just a lot of meaningless squiggles.

"Similar. We didn't actually see any works by this artist. But you know what? Tomorrow let's drive down to Los Angeles, and I'll take you to a couple of museums there. There are some really great works at the Museum of Contemporary Art."

"OK," Lila agreed happily. "Do you think we'll have time for a little shopping?"

Robby grinned at her. "Anything you want, sweetie."

"That's what I like to hear," Lila purred.

"You're bad," Robby teased softly. "But seriously, what should we do for dinner? I'd like to take you someplace nice."

"How about the Carousel? They have great seafood. I haven't been there in a while."

Robby lay back in his lounge chair. "Sounds good."

"Rats!" Jessica flung down the fifth outfit she had tried on. Nothing she had was special enough. Jeremy had already seen her black linen two-piece.

Suddenly a lot of her clothes seemed too young, too trendy, too obvious. Jeremy was an older guy. He had been dating real women for years—women who were all older than Jessica.

Sighing, she flopped down on her bed. She had an hour until Bruce came to get her. *He'd better not be late.* Sue and Jeremy, who were now taking a drive through Sweet Valley, planned to be at the Carousel at seven. She and Bruce would arrive at seven fifteen. Sue had never seen Bruce, so she wouldn't know that the whole thing was a sham. If Jeremy was suspicious about why Jessica was out on a date with the person who was so hateful to her at the mall, she would just explain it away as a lover's quarrel.

Finally Jessica got up and decided to raid Elizabeth's closet. Usually Jessica thought Elizabeth dressed too frumpily, but as she wasn't having any luck with her own wardrobe . . .

Wrinkling her nose at the perpetual neatness of Elizabeth's room, Jessica strode to the closet and started riffling through clothes. White palazzo pants? No. Sheer baby-doll dress over leggings? No. Fitted coral suit? No.

"Ah!" Jessica pulled out a dress that Elizabeth had worn to Enid's sweet-sixteen party.

"Not bad," she murmured to her reflection once she had slipped into the strapless sheath. The dress was of a deep aquamarine silk, and was long and slim and fitted, an elastic back holding the smooth

86

bodice in place. Jessica turned sideways, sucked in her stomach, then turned back again. She looked slender and delicate—just the effect she wanted. Then she tried on the short bolero jacket that went over it, of the same aquamarine silk, piped in white. *The perfect touch.* Shimmying out of the dress, Jessica placed it carefully on Elizabeth's bed and then began scrambling through the closet, looking for the matching shoes. "Gotcha!" she cried, pulling out a pair of un-Elizabeth-like high heels.

Then she ran to the shower.

At seven o'clock Bruce pulled up to the Wakefield house in his black Porsche. Out of habit he smoothed his dark hair back with one hand as he dropped his Ray-Bans on the console between the front seats. Frowning, he checked his watch and glanced at the front door.

"If that dizzy blond isn't ready, so help me, I'm taking off," he muttered. "Of all the asinine plans . . ." He continued to grumble as he walked up the path to the front door. He'd barely touched the doorbell before the door opened and there was Jessica, in a softly clinging silk dress, her face glowing with happy anticipation.

Bruce swallowed and took a step back. For just an instant, he could see why Jessica usually had some hapless male buzzing around her. *OK, so maybe they're not total idiots.* And he remembered those few crazy weeks when she had looked that way for him all the time. . . . But that strong personality— *Wake up*, he told himself. He still had a bad taste in his mouth from their explosive battle of wills.

But he couldn't deny she looked totally hot tonight.

"Wakefield," he said evenly. "Not bad."

"Thanks. You look very . . . suitable . . . yourself." Turning, Jessica leaned back into the house and yelled, "Bye! I'm going out!" Then she slammed the door and skipped down the walkway before her parents could question her.

Chapter 8

"OK, Wakefield, OK. No need to go overboard," Bruce said through clenched teeth.

Jessica gave him a teasing smile. "I'm not going overboard," she purred, looking at him lovingly. "I'm just trying not to make them suspicious." Picking up her water glass, she took a deep drink, gazing at Bruce over the rim.

"Fine. Just quit looking at me as though I'm a fly and you're a largemouth bass." Bruce irritably opened his menu and began to peruse the list.

"Hmmm—the tournedos of beef are excellent here," Jessica said, projecting her voice so that Sue and Jeremy, seated just a few tables away, could hear. "I just adore this place. It makes me feel so rich and pampered." Then she looked hard into Bruce's eyes and lowered her voice. "It's hard *not* to look at you as though you're a fly, Bruce."

"You're buying, huh?" Bruce murmured through an affectionate grin in keeping with his role.

"Yes. So?" Jessica narrowed her eyes.

"The steak," Bruce told the waiter decisively. "The filet mignon with the mushroom and pepper sauce, cooked rare. And I'll have the oysters to begin with—are they good now?"

"Yes, sir. We have them flown in from Oregon," the waiter said.

"Fine. How about the *pommes Anna,* a small house salad on the side, and sparkling cider for the lady and myself," Bruce concluded cheerfully.

Jessica glared at him. If they made it through this meal, she was going to strangle him. Probably right outside in the parking lot. Maybe in the foyer of the restaurant. That is, if she weren't too weak from eating next-to-nothing to compensate for his feast.

"And for the lady?" the waiter prompted.

"Um, I'll have the chicken consomme to begin," she said, scanning the menu. *Drat, even chicken broth is expensive.* "And then the dinner-size portion of the *salade nicoise.*"

The waiter took their menus deferentially and bustled off.

"You would *think,*" Jessica hissed across the table at Bruce, "that if nothing else, you'd appreciate getting a nice free meal out of this. But nooo. You have to push it with your steak and your oysters. How does Pam stand you? She must be broke by now, you greedy pig!"

Bruce smirked at her across the table. "Pam gets me for free," he said smugly, leaning over and caressing her hand. "You, Wakefield, have to pay for the pleasure of my company. Now wipe that unbecoming look off your face and smile. Your friend's watching."

Biting back her retort, Jessica looked up to find Sue waving at her gaily. Looking from her to Jeremy, Jessica saw his dark eyes glaring at hers, and her heart beat with a little thump. He looked jealous, she realized with elation. Jealous of Bruce. *A very, very good sign.*

"Bruce, you selfish jerk," Jessica cooed, edging closer to him. "Every day I wake up and thank God I came to my senses about you. My only regret is that we ever dated at all."

Bruce reached over and caressed her cheek. "At last we agree on something, Wakefield." He laughed softly and brought her hand to his lips, pretending to kiss it. From the corner of her eye, Jessica saw Sue grinning at her conspiratorially. Jeremy's face looked like a storm cloud.

"Careful, Bruce," Jessica whispered, smiling. "I have to *eat* with that hand." She gracefully pulled her hand away and folded it primly in her lap.

The waiter brought their first courses then, and opened the bottle of sparkling cider with great ceremony. Jessica raised her glass to Sue and Jeremy. *Here's to your engagement, Jeremy, sweetheart.* Sue returned the gesture cheerfully, but Jeremy barely raised his own glass. *He must really think Bruce is my date,* she thought with delight.

"Jessica!" Lila's surprised voice brought Jessica out of her reverie. "And—Bruce?" Lila's eyes were almost popping with disbelief. Instantly her face took on a sly, mocking expression. "Now, if you were here with *Elizabeth,* I might understand, but . . ."

"Shut up, Fowler," Bruce growled. "Quit proving you're as much of an airhead as you look. Jessica and I are here just as friends."

"I'll explain it all to you later, Lila," Jessica put in quickly. "It's a long story."

"It always is with you, Jess," Lila returned knowingly.

"Anyway, what are you doing here?" Jessica asked.

"Robby and I came for a bite to eat," Lila said casually. "He's dealing with the valet parking or something. Listen, we're going to sit by ourselves, but maybe later we can have dessert together or something."

"Sure, whatever," Jessica said.

Just then Robby Goodman came in, and Lila introduced him to Bruce. After shaking Bruce's hand, he turned to Jessica. "I remember you from the beach that day." He looked concerned by the memory.

"Robby, look," Lila broke in. "It's your friend from New York, sitting with Sue."

"Hey, you're right! Come on, Lila, I'll introduce you. Excuse us."

As Robby led her to Jeremy's table, Lila gave Jessica a quick, meaningful look before turning to say hello to Jeremy and Sue.

Of course Jessica had told Lila the whole sad story, and she sighed with relief to know that her friend was here and on her side. *Just don't tell Robby the real story about me and Bruce,* she silently willed her friend.

"That girl's blind date is from New York?" Bruce said skeptically. "Kind of far to come for a date, isn't it?"

"Just eat," Jessica said. "There's no point in explaining it."

Their meal progressed smoothly and according to plan. Jeremy glanced up just as Bruce gave Jessica a bite of his filet mignon. "Mmmm," she murmured, staring into Bruce's eyes as her lips closed around the fork.

"Oh, please, Wakefield," Bruce groaned, rolling his eyes. "Spare me."

Jessica abruptly switched the conversation to their summer vacations, and they managed to get through the meal without snapping each other's heads off.

"That was fabulous, Wakefield," Bruce said, pushing back his empty plate. "Of course, I come here pretty often, but I'm always happy to eat another of the Carousel's filets."

"I can hear your arteries clogging from over here," Jessica said dryly.

"Now, where's our waiter? I think they have my favorite chocolate cake as the special dessert tonight."

"Dessert? How can you possibly eat dessert after that heavy meal? Oh, I forgot. You still have your head to fill," she said resentfully. *I'm getting more broke by the minute,* she thought.

Bruce glared at her. "Careful. I could just walk out of here, and then your friend would have to muddle through her 'blind date' with only you."

"I'm sorry," Jessica said stiffly. The last thing she wanted was to have Jeremy see Bruce storm out on her. That wouldn't give him too much to be jealous of.

Bruce smiled. "Whoa, this must be important for you to grovel like that so willingly. I wonder what else it would be worth your while to do for me?"

"Don't let your limited imagination run away with you," Jessica said sweetly. "What would you like for dessert?"

Bruce signalled to their waiter, who returned with two dessert menus.

I wonder what Jeremy and Sue are up to? Jessica wondered, glancing oh-so-casually around the restaurant. A fluffy piece of cake sat between them, but they didn't touch it. Instead, Jeremy took both of Sue's hands in his. He seemed to be speaking to her very earnestly, and Sue's face glowed radiantly. Clearly, he spoke words she wanted to hear.

94

Then Jeremy reached one hand down to the pocket of his jacket. This was it. He was about to present Sue with her engagement ring.

Jessica felt a dry lump form in her throat. The love of her life was formalizing his commitment to another woman right under her nose. *This can't be happening.* . . . Not knowing what she was doing, she jumped up and headed toward their table.

"Jessica, what are you doing? Sit down!"

Turning to face Bruce, Jessica plastered a smile on her perfectly made-up face. "Let's go have dessert with Sue and Jeremy," she said sweetly. "Come *on,* Bruce."

Reluctantly Bruce threw down his napkin and followed her across the restaurant, taking his cider with him.

"Sue, Jeremy, hi," Jessica said brightly, standing beside them. "How was your dinner? Isn't this a romantic place? Bruce and I love it, don't we?" She nudged Bruce in the ribs sharply.

"Oof—yeah, it's great," Bruce agreed, tightening his grip on her elbow painfully.

Jeremy's hand had dropped away from his pocket and was back on the table. *That's it, Jeremy. You don't really want to give her that, do you?*

"Why don't you join us for dessert?" Sue asked.

"Love to," Jessica agreed instantly, sitting down between Sue and Jeremy. Bruce stalked to the other side of the table and sat down stiffly, sending Jessica a warning look.

"Bruce Patman," Bruce introduced himself,

shaking Jeremy's hand, then Sue's.

"Sue Gibbons, and this is my fiancé, Jeremy Randall," Sue explained.

"Fiancé?" Bruce repeated, a confused look on his face.

"Hmmm, what do I want for dessert?" Jessica said quickly, looking down at the dessert menu.

"Um-hmm," Sue answered Bruce. "We're getting married in less than a month. Jessica and Elizabeth have been so sweet to me, helping me plan the wedding. Of course, if you're Jessica's boyfriend, we'd love to have you join us at the ceremony."

Bruce practically choked on his cider. Jessica shot him a poisonous glance. "Do be careful, sweetheart. Did it go down the wrong tube?" She turned to Sue. "Bruce might be busy that day, but we'll see. Won't we, sweetie?"

Bruce gave Jessica a dangerously innocent smile. "Yeah. We'll talk about it *later*," he said.

"So, how long have you been dating?" Jeremy suddenly asked Bruce.

"Excuse me?" Bruce asked, trying to catch Jessica's eye.

"I said, how long have you been dating Jessica?" Jeremy repeated.

Bruce frowned. "Not long."

"I hope you know what a special thing you have. I mean, Jessica has been really great to Sue. It shows she's a fine person. I hope you realize that," Jeremy said quickly.

Jessica sucked in her breath. *A fine person? How about a fine kisser?*

"Oh, sure. Wake— I mean, *Jessica's* a peach. Everyone knows that," Bruce said in a bored tone.

"Sue and Jessica are practically family," Jeremy plowed on. "I'd be very upset if I thought anyone would hurt a member of Sue's family." He gave Bruce a cold, threatening glare.

Now he's sounding possessive, Jessica thought, both thrilled and angry. *He doesn't want me himself, but he doesn't want anyone else to have me, either!*

"What happens between Jessica and myself is none of your business," Bruce said in a low, hard tone.

"Not if she gets hurt," Jeremy said obstinately, ignoring Sue's anxious patting of his arm.

"Jer, honey," she was saying.

"She can take it," Bruce said coldly. "She's a big girl."

"I think you'd better—" Jeremy began.

"Oh, please, Jeremy," Jessica said laughingly. "Like Bruce said, I'm a big girl. Besides, Bruce and I have an . . . understanding," she said in a husky, sexy voice. "Isn't that right, Bruce?"

"Yeah. I understand that if you don't leave with me right now, there's going to be major trouble." He glared at Jeremy.

"Certainly, Bruce," Jessica cooed, getting to her feet in a fluid, easy motion that caused her dress to sway and cling in all the right places. "Lead the way. Jeremy—so good to see you again.

Sue, I'll see you back at the house. 'Night."

Well, not bad, Jessica thought once she settled into Bruce's black Porsche. She'd kept Jeremy from giving Sue the ring, at least for a little while, *and* she'd made him jealous. Of *Bruce.* She stifled a giggle.

"You want to tell me what that was about?" Bruce finally ground out as his car sped through the dark hills of Sweet Valley.

"Why, I don't know," Jessica said innocently. "I mean, he was acting like he was my father—or my husband."

"He's going to be acting like roadkill if he doesn't watch out," Bruce said grimly, rounding a hairpin turn. "And whatever happened to your blind date story? You've been helping her plan the wedding! What kind of game are you playing, Wakefield?"

Her mind whirring, Jessica improvised. "That's just it, Bruce," she said, trying to sound forlorn. "Sue's been staying with us, and Elizabeth and I have been swamped with wedding this and wedding that. And you know I don't have a boyfriend—I haven't had one since Sam. I just couldn't bear to have Sue feeling sorry for me because she has a real, live fiancé, and I hardly even date. Much. I thought if I showed her I could go out with one of the handsomest, sexiest, richest boys in town, she wouldn't think I was so pathetic." Jessica tried to look humble and admiring.

Bruce snorted, but the anger had left his face. He had bought it.

Are there no limits to his ego? In the secure, secluded darkness of Bruce's car, Jessica allowed herself a smile.

"Well, Wakefield, it's been real, and it's been fun, but it hasn't been real fun," Bruce said dryly as he parked in front of her house on Calico Drive.

Jessica laughed. "I'm sorry I took you out under false pretenses, and I'm sorry about Jeremy—I can't imagine what got into him," she lied. "At least you had a good dinner, right?"

"Right," Bruce said, turning to grin at her reluctantly. "I guess I did. Where are you going to take me next time?"

Jessica made a mock grimace. "You wish. Honestly, Bruce Patman—I'd almost think you *like* being a boy toy."

He looked outraged for a moment, then broke into laughter. "Wakefield, you're a total lunatic, but no one can say you're boring. Now go on, get out of here. I want to call Pam before it's too late."

"OK," Jessica said cheerfully. "Later, Bruce." She opened her car door to get out.

"One more thing, Jess."

She turned around. "Now what?"

"You looked great tonight," Bruce said quietly.

Jessica searched his face. Amazing—no sarcasm there. Unthinkingly, she leaned back and gave him a quick, hard kiss on the mouth. Then she jumped out of the car and slammed her door shut.

Ol' Patman and I are two of a kind, she mused as she let herself in the front door. *Which is precisely why we don't get along. But he was a real pal tonight. A whiny, suspicious pal, whose grossly expensive dinner I'm going to be paying off for a long time, but a pal nevertheless.*

Chapter 9

That *was sleep?* Jessica grumbled silently as she dragged herself downstairs early the next morning. Bad dreams about Jeremy and their ill-fated love had kept her tossing all night. Her parents, Elizabeth, and Sue were all in the breakfast nook of the kitchen when she came in.

"Goodness, what time is it?" Mrs. Wakefield looked at her watch in alarm. "Oh, I thought I was late. But you're early," she told Jessica cheerfully.

"Uh-huh." Jessica groped her way to the fridge and took out the milk, then somehow managed to get down a bowl and a box of cereal. She pried her eyes open enough to read the label. "Don't we have any cereal that isn't good for you?" she complained. "I need something with sugar and artificial coloring to help me get going in the morning."

Her family laughed.

"Toast, Jessica?" her father offered. "I'm making myself some."

"No, thanks." Plunking herself down at her place, she filled her bowl with cereal and milk. Mechanically she took a bite and started chewing. And chewing. And chewing. "What's in this stuff? Wood fibers? It's not even getting soggy."

"Someone got up on the wrong side of the bed this morning," Elizabeth observed annoyingly.

"What of it?" Jessica snarled, turning to read the comics in the *Sweet Valley News*.

Sue laughed and poured a glass of juice. "Well, I think it's a beautiful morning," she said. "The best morning of my entire life, in fact."

Sue waved her left hand in front of Jessica's face. Jessica saw a streak of flashing light.

"Notice anything different?" Sue asked.

Jessica felt dizzy as she stared at the huge, sparkling diamond on Sue's third finger.

"Isn't that a beautiful ring, Jessica?" Mrs. Wakefield prompted.

"Yes, beautiful," Jessica said, watching it flash in the sunlight streaming through the kitchen window. Struggling to remember her manners, she forced herself to smile at Sue. "It's gorgeous, Sue. Do you like it?"

"You know I do—it's the one I picked out. But I'm even happier about what it represents—that Jeremy and I are committed to each other, and to each other alone. I almost feel married already."

Her smile was as brilliant as her diamond.

"That's great," Jessica said, turning back to her cereal.

"I was so thrilled when Jeremy gave it to me last night—I almost cried. I guess that sounds silly."

"No, it doesn't sound silly at all," Jessica said slowly.

"I'm so happy for you, dear," Mrs. Wakefield said, coming over to give Sue a hug. "And I know your mother would be very happy too. And now," she said, glancing at her watch, "I better get to the office. Girls, I've volunteered you to help Sue pick out a wedding dress today. I'm sure you'll find something special. I only wish I could come too—if I weren't so busy . . ."

"Don't worry, Mom. It'll be fun to help Sue find a dress. I think we'll start with the bridal department at Lytton & Brown, and then work our way across town," Elizabeth said.

"Good plan. I've got to run now. See you guys later." Mrs. Wakefield swept out of the kitchen, her perfume trailing behind her.

"I better go too," Mr. Wakefield said, taking a last sip of coffee. "Have fun, girls."

"Bye, Dad." Elizabeth waved her bagel at him.

When their parents were gone, Elizabeth said, "I wish you two could have been with me yesterday—we had such a good time. By the end of the evening I felt closer to my friends than ever before. Talk about the strength of the sisterhood—wow. I couldn't get over all the feelings that bubbled up to the surface once we started delving."

Sounds like a blast—a smorgasbord of sisterhood, Jessica thought, practically spraining her jaw on her healthy cereal.

"Good for you, Elizabeth," Sue said approvingly. "It must have been so exciting, getting that kind of support from your peers."

"It was. I mean, I feel so empowered now," Elizabeth went on enthusiastically. "We each brought a self-help book to discuss. I brought *Real Women, Bad Men*. Enid had *Attracting the Love You Want*. Penny Ayala talked about *Primal Woman, Woman of Strength*. Cheryl Thomas had one that focused on issues for African-American women. It was just fascinating," Elizabeth raved. "We sat in a big circle on Enid's floor, and it was like being surrounded by love, you know? After last night, I feel as if I can do anything."

"Wow, that sounds fabulous," Sue agreed. "I wish I could have gone—although I'm glad I didn't," she joked, looking at her ring again. "So did you feel as though there was one particular book that spoke to you the most?"

"Well, I really think maybe it was the *Primal Woman* one. It made the most sense, and was really focused on getting your own act together before you do anything else. I just related to it. If I had felt strong within myself last month, I never would have gotten involved with Luke in London.

I see that now. But from this moment on, I'm taking the reins of my life—I'm responsible for me. My destiny is in my hands." Elizabeth waved her banana dramatically to illustrate her point.

"'I am woman, hear me roar. . . .'" Jessica started singing through a mouthful of her cereal. "As I lay down on Enid's floor . . ."

"Laugh if you must, Jessica, but I know I'm doing the right thing in getting in touch with my primal woman."

"Shouldn't you wait for Todd to come home for that?" Jessica asked.

"Very funny. I'm splitting my sides," Elizabeth said dryly. She got up to put her dishes in the sink. "As soon as you slither out of the shower, call us and we'll hit the mall." Then she stalked off into the den.

"I don't know," Sue said, gazing at herself in the three-way mirror. It was early afternoon, and they had already checked out every wedding dress at Lytton & Brown. Sue hadn't liked any of them. After a quick lunch at the food court in the mall, they had come to Bridal Glory, a new brides-only shop. Now Sue was wearing a floor-length, cream-colored dress with a sweetheart-neckline. She was frowning.

"Do you have anything less . . . traditional?" she asked the salesclerk. "I'm getting married on the beach, and I think a long dress wouldn't work very well."

"The beach—how romantic," the salesclerk said. "I think maybe over here . . ." She bustled off to get some other dresses for Sue to look at.

"How about this one?" Jessica said, holding up a dress she had found near the window. It had a huge bow across the back, and two more on each sleeve. It looked as though a flock of enormous white butterflies had decided to nest on the dress.

"Oh, Jess, no," Sue laughed. "It's awful. You're such a kidder. That must be the fourth horrible dress you've shown me."

Jessica glumly took the dress back to its rack. Catching sight of her reflection in a store mirror, she was startled by the look of despair she saw in her eyes. *First the ring, and now this. An actual wedding dress.* There was going to be an actual wedding. Sighing, Jessica wished again that Sue would choose a laughable dress, a hideous dress that would make Jeremy realize his mistake and call the wedding to a halt.

"What's the matter with you?" Elizabeth hissed in her ear as Sue changed into another gown. "You've been moping all morning. Now you keep pushing horrible dresses at Sue. You better get it together, Jess. You don't want Sue to have any suspicions, do you? You're lucky she hasn't picked up on any vibes so far."

"What vibes? There's nothing to be suspicious about. Jeremy's made it perfectly clear that he's going to marry her—even though he loves *me*. I know he does, Liz."

"Look, Jess, Jeremy is engaged to Sue. He must love her. It's not her fault that you have a bad crush on him. You have to promise me you won't let her know—it would ruin her wedding. Whatever happened between you and Jeremy, Sue doesn't deserve that. She's so nice, and so eager to have a settled home of her own."

Jessica looked into Elizabeth's earnest expression. "I know, Liz. And if it were anyone but Jeremy, I would be thrilled for her. But it's not a bad crush, Liz. I'm totally in love with him. We were meant to be together."

"Who? That cute boy you were with last night?"

Sue's cheerful inquiry made the sisters whirl around.

"What?" Elizabeth yelped.

"Here, zip me up," Sue asked, presenting her back. "That cute boy you were with last night, Jessica. Is that who you're in love with?"

Elizabeth pulled up Sue's zipper. "Cute boy, Jessica?" Eyebrows raised, she turned to face her sister.

"Yes, that's who I meant," Jessica said, giving Elizabeth a panicked look.

"What cute boy?" Elizabeth asked again.

Sue turned to face them, and smoothed her dress with her hands. "What do you two think? Too much?"

"Oh, Sue, I love it," Elizabeth said, forgetting her concern over Jessica's mystery date. "That's really you."

Sue wore a white flowing gown, tightly fitted through the bodice. The neckline was a low sweetheart, a bit of delicate lace trimming the top, and the hem was cut gracefully along the bias.

"You look fabulous," Elizabeth said admiringly. "Doesn't she, Jess?"

Jessica had to admit that she did. "It's a great dress, Sue. I think it's perfect."

"With a choker of pearls, and maybe some dangly earrings," Elizabeth started to paint the whole picture.

"And maybe some low heels out of matching silk?" Sue suggested.

"That's it. That's the one." Elizabeth gave Sue a spontaneous hug. "You're going to be the most beautiful bride Sweet Valley has seen in years!" She and Sue laughed together, hugging.

Sue pulled back to include Jessica in the hug. "I know you guys have done so much for me already," she said, her eyes shining. "But I have another big favor to ask."

"Anything," Elizabeth promised.

"Will you both be my bridesmaids? I mean, I don't have any sisters. I have some good friends in New York, but my very best friend won't be able to make it. I know it's asking a lot, but it would really mean a lot to me. I feel as though you're *almost* my sisters."

"Oh, Sue," Elizabeth said, hugging her again. "You know we'd love to. Right, Jess?"

Jessica looked back at Elizabeth, wide-eyed. *Now you're pushing me too far,* her gaze said.

"Right, Jess?" Elizabeth said again, a warning tone in her voice.

"Of course." Jessica smiled at Sue, she hoped convincingly. "We'd love to."

"Oh, great!" Sue said, bouncing up and down. "That's a big relief. Now I better go tell the salesclerk I want this dress. I think it might need a little altering." She skipped off to find the clerk.

"Ugh, she looked fabulous," Jessica moaned despondently. "And now I have to be a bridesmaid on the worst day of my life."

"She really did, and you really do," Elizabeth agreed. She linked her arm through her sister's. "Jessica, please. For your own sake. Please try to forget you ever met Jeremy, OK?"

"It's no use, Liz. He's already burned his way into my heart," Jessica said sadly.

Sue came back, her face radiant. "I knew you two would help me find the perfect dress! I can't wait for Jeremy to see me in it. Would you guys mind if I just took a look at some headpieces while we're here?"

"Of course not." Elizabeth laughed. "Go ahead."

Sue darted off to another department, and Elizabeth turned solemn eyes on Jessica. "Jess, they're really getting married."

"I know," Jessica said dully. "They're really getting married."

"Try to pull yourself together, OK? We have to go to the caterers with her tomorrow. And soon we'll have to go shopping for our own bridesmaid dresses."

Jessica sighed and looked at her twin. "I'll do it somehow. I don't know how, but I'll just try to get through it."

"By the way, who *was* the mysterious cute boy you had a date with last night?"

Jessica rolled her eyes. "Bruce Patman. Don't ask. It's a long story."

"I can't hold still much longer," Lila warned Robby.

"OK—just another minute. I just need to get your eyes down," Robby said, sketching rapidly. "OK. You can relax."

Lila collapsed backward on the couch in her palatial living room. "Thank goodness. I think I have a permanent crick in my neck."

Laughing, Robby came over to the couch and slid his hands under her shoulders. "Sit up and I'll rub your poor neck."

"Mmmm." Lila immediately sat up and turned around. Soon Robby's strong hands were unknotting all the tense muscles in her neck and back. "Oh, that feels so good," Lila murmured. "You're an artist at this, as well as a regular artist. Now let me see it. Can I?"

"Sure." Robby went and picked up the

110

stretched canvas he had been working on in charcoal. He turned it around with a flourish. "Ta-daa."

Gazing at the sketched likeness of herself, Lila marveled again at Robby's talent. She had seen other drawings and paintings of his, of course, but this was of *her*. Even in the preliminary sketch, Robby seemed to have captured her very soul on canvas.

Lila threw her arms around Robby. "I love it! You're brilliant!"

Robby hugged her back. "It's easy with a subject as beautiful as you."

"I can't wait to see the final painting," Lila said, cuddling next to Robby on the couch.

"If you can bear to pose again for it, Knot-Neck."

"I won't even mind," she promised him. "I can't wait to see the final painting. I know Mother and Dad are going to love it. It's so exciting to know such a talented artist."

Taking her hand, Robby looked into her eyes. "What if I were a penniless artist?" he asked lightly. "What if all I had in the world was my talent? Would you still care about me?"

Lila felt as though she was drowning in his loving gaze. "Of course I would, Robby. But the best part is, you're not penniless. You'll never have to starve in a garret in Paris while you wait to be discovered—you could stay in a suite at the Louis Quinze."

"Do you agree that what's really important is for

111

us to be together, and that everything else—any fact about our lives—is irrelevant?" Leaning closer, he nuzzled her neck softly. A tingle of anticipation ran down Lila's spine.

"Of course I do," she breathed. "Compared to our being together, nothing else matters." She lifted her lips to Robby's, and he kissed her, gently but with a growing ardor that made Lila's head swim.

"I think I'm falling in love, Lila," she heard Robby murmur against her neck.

A delighted thrill shook her. "I think I'm falling in love too, Robby."

"Hi, sweetie. Do you miss me?" Todd's familiar voice came over the phone. It sounded like heaven to Elizabeth's ears.

"You know I do," she said huskily, dragging the phone into her bedroom and nudging the door shut with her foot.

"I'm not catching you in the middle of dinner, am I?" he asked. "I keep forgetting it's an hour earlier there."

"No, we finished a while ago. How's your grandmother? I haven't spoken to you in, oh . . . about two days," Elizabeth teased him. Todd had been calling so regularly that Jessica was complaining it was as though he had never left. And he knew every detail of the wedding saga.

"She's doing pretty well. Mom's been helping

her redecorate the living room. My dad and I are mostly just going to movies, going bowling, stuff like that, to stay out of the way. What have you been doing?"

"This and that. Jess and I have been helping Sue sort out details for the wedding. And I've just been hanging out with my girlfriends. We've been getting together to work on a mini self-improvement course, sort of."

"Oh? I can't imagine that there's anything to improve about you, Elizabeth," Todd teased gently.

Elizabeth smiled into the phone. One of the best things about Todd was that he had always accepted her the way she was, through thick and thin, good times and bad. "You'd be surprised," she said. "I got pretty shook up in London, and it made me realize I need to get back in touch with my deepest feelings. Really explore my own sense of womanhood."

"Hmmm," Todd said noncommittally. "Well, I'm sure you know what's best for you. Can I do anything to help?"

"I'll let you know." Elizabeth giggled. "But the point of it is that I sort of have to do it alone."

"But you said you and your friends had been doing this together." Todd sounded confused.

"*Girl*friends. It's different."

"Liz, I thought I was your best friend, besides your boyfriend."

Elizabeth thought for a moment. It was true

113

that Todd was usually the one she would automatically turn to when she had a problem, but there *were* some things she would tell only Enid, because she was a girl and had that special girls-only understanding.

"In almost every way you are, Todd. But there are some things that women just have to stick together on, without letting romance get in the way."

"Why is it that I feel like if I said that about guys, you would call me sexist?" Todd sounded hurt.

"Todd! When have I ever called you sexist?" Elizabeth protested.

"When have I ever given you cause to?" he countered.

Taking a deep breath, Elizabeth flopped down on her bed. "Look, Todd, I don't want to argue with you, and I don't want to hurt your feelings. I miss you and I want you to come home soon, OK? The summer's rushing by, and I want to be able to have some fun together before it's over."

"I want that too," Todd agreed softly.

"Will you be home in time for the wedding?"

"Oh, sure. In plenty of time. How's Jessica behaving?"

"Pretty good, so far. But you know Jessica . . ."

"She's like a bomb waiting to go off," Todd agreed with a chuckle. "Well, tell her not to start the fireworks without me, OK?"

"I'm trying to keep her from starting the fireworks at all," Elizabeth said dryly. "But now we have to be Sue's bridesmaids, and it worries me. I have nightmares about Jessica tripping Sue on the way to the altar, or screaming out something when the minister asks if anyone has any objections."

Todd's warm laugh filled her ears. "Unfortunately, with Jessica, any of those possibilities are only too likely. Just try to keep her on a short leash."

"Yeah, right. I've always been *so* successful doing that with her. Look, just hurry home, OK? I'm going to need all the help I can get."

"OK. It won't be long now. Hang in there. I'll talk to you soon. Love you."

"I love you too, Todd." *That's one thing I've always been sure of, isn't it?* Elizabeth thought as she hung up the phone.

Chapter 10

"This is one of my favorite beaches," Elizabeth said on Thursday morning. She and Sue were deciding upon a likely spot for the wedding.

"It's beautiful," Sue agreed. "What is its name again?"

"Moon Beach. It even has a romantic name. And it's not too far from Sweet Valley."

Sue walked along the sand, looking out over the ocean. "Elizabeth—what if it rains?" Suddenly she looked panicked. "I was talking to my best friend in New York last night—her name is Stacy, you'd really like her—and she reminded me how risky it is to have the wedding on the beach. Maybe we should go ahead and have it in the cathedral downtown. And we could have the reception at the country club."

"Relax. I already thought of that. We'll rent a

117

tent, and have them set it up here on the beach. Then, if it rains, which it hardly ever does," Elizabeth said, "we'll all just move into the tent. But if you'd really rather have it in a church . . ."

Sue looked doubtful. "Well, it just seems as though it would be easier. But I know Jeremy has his heart set on having it on the beach. So I guess that's what we'll do. It's so hard to know what to decide." She grimaced. "It's times like this that I really miss my mom. She would have been great at this."

"Do you have any aunts or cousins that you're close to?" Elizabeth asked.

Sue shook her head. "Both my parents are only children. My dad is really great—you'll meet him at the wedding. And I have good friends, besides Stacy, I mean. I've been talking to her almost every night, telling her what's going on. And practically the whole office at Project Nature is coming, and so are a lot of my friends from the boarding school I went to. But it's just not the same. That's why I've been so grateful to have Jeremy—he sort of fills in the empty spaces, you know? He's so wonderful, he's even paying for the wedding himself." She blinked and brushed her hand across her eyes.

Elizabeth patted her shoulder. "I know how much you love him. But Sue, if the beach isn't what you want, maybe you should talk to Jeremy about it. Maybe you two can compromise."

"Oh, no—it's fine, really. What Jeremy wants, I want. I just love him so much. I want him to be happy all the time. And a wedding on the beach would be really pretty. I've just never been to one."

"If you're sure . . . See, I was thinking that we'd enclose little maps with each invitation, explaining how to get here. Then we'd have the tent over here—" She gestured to the left. "—and the band over here. The caterers could set up their tables in a sort of semicircle, so that people could mingle."

"OK, I'm convinced!" Sue said with a laugh. "You could make a wedding at a zoo sound like a great idea, Elizabeth. So it's decided. Now, do you really think *this* is exactly the right beach? Maybe we should look at one or two others, just to make sure. That is, if you don't mind. I know I'm running you ragged—and we still have to meet Jeremy at the caterers in a little while."

Elizabeth patted Sue on the back. "It's no problem, Sue, really. I'd love to show you another beach. Let's head back to the Jeep."

"What color would you like, Miss?"

Jessica drifted out of her daydream. "Hmm?"

The manicurist pointed at Jessica's left hand. "For your nails. What color polish would you like?"

"Oh, sorry. Let's see . . ." Jessica tried to second-guess what she would be wearing over the

119

next few days, but even the thought of clothes didn't excite her. "How about your basic pinky-peach?" she suggested. "But not too light."

She sat back in her chair and absentmindedly sank into a daydream as the manicurist expertly applied polish to her nails. This morning she had awakened feeling so unloved and depressed that she had decided a facial and a manicure were in order to cheer herself up. Usually Lila could be counted on to come with her, but lately she had hardly seen her best friend. Lila had sure struck it rich with *her* stranger. It seemed so unfair that all the romantic happiness was reserved for her, and for Sue. . . .

By the time Jessica walked back home, she was feeling hot and sticky. *Still, it's better than being stuck at the beach with Elizabeth and Little Miss Bride,* she supposed. She decided to take a dip in the pool to cool off.

"Jessica! Jessica!"

Surfacing after her dive underwater, Jessica shook her wet hair out of her eyes and looked for the voice. Her mother was standing by the sliding glass doors leading to the kitchen. She looked frantic.

Jessica swam quickly to the side of the pool. "What's wrong, Mom? How come you're home in the middle of the day?"

"Thank goodness you're here. I had some free time today, so I was going to show Jeremy where the caterer is—we're supposed to meet Sue and Elizabeth there in half an hour."

Jessica climbed out of the pool and stood dripping next to her mother on the patio. She grabbed her long blond hair with both hands and started to wring it out.

"Careful, honey, don't splash me," Mrs. Wakefield said, stepping back.

"Sorry. So what's the problem?" Suddenly Jessica froze as Jeremy stepped out of the kitchen onto the patio. *Of course he shows up when I'm shivering in this white maillot, while he's dry and fully clothed. He always has the upper hand.*

"The problem is that I've just been called to a meeting—it's the only time the client can meet me before she goes out of town. Can you do me a favor and go with Jeremy to the caterers? We thought we'd use Michael's—they did a great job at the Wilkinses' anniversary party. But you know they're on that little back road on the hill behind the mall; it's a little tricky to get to. So can you get dressed and direct Jeremy there? He has his rental car."

"Really, Mrs. Wakefield, I can probably just find it myself. I'd hate to interrupt Jessica's swim," Jeremy put in.

"Oh, it's no trouble, Jeremy," Jessica said airily. "It *is* sort of tucked away. I'd be happy to show you."

"That's my girl," Mrs. Wakefield said, happily patting Jessica's cheek. "I have to dash—see you

121

tonight!" With that she practically flew through the doors to the kitchen, and a minute later Jessica heard her mother's car engine start.

"Let me just go change," Jessica said, walking toward the house.

"I'll wait here," Jeremy told her, sitting down stiffly on one of the patio chairs.

Ten minutes later, Jessica had showered and changed into a cool summer dress that had a long, floaty skirt that hovered just above her ankles. She'd loosely tied her still-damp blond hair in a ribbon, and delicate gold earrings dangled from her ears. *At least I look cooler than I feel,* she thought, surveying her image in the mirror. Her skin was glowing healthily, and her nails looked great. The peachy-pink was a good idea.

Soon she was settled beside Jeremy in his car, adjusting the air conditioner vents to blow directly on her.

"You'll catch cold. Your hair's still wet," Jeremy said, backing out of the Wakefields' driveway.

"Germs cause colds, not wet hair," Jessica said breezily, looking out the window. "First thing you want to do is go to the end of Calico Drive, then take a left."

Jessica had been to Michael's at least three times and remembered exactly how to get there. But Jeremy didn't know that. They drove in silence through the pretty tree-lined streets of Sweet Valley. Finally, Jeremy said, "You didn't have to do

122

this, you know. I could have called them and asked for directions."

"It's OK. I wasn't doing anything else." Jessica managed to inject just the right touch of boredom into her voice.

"You didn't have a date?"

"Uh-uh," she said, not missing a beat. "He was . . . busy. OK, take a right at the top of this hill."

"Sweet Valley really is one of the prettier cities I've ever seen."

"Yes, it is," Jessica agreed proudly. "I love living here. Take another right at the light."

"Miller's Point?" Jeremy asked after following her directions. "What is this place?"

Jessica looked around, affecting confusion. "I don't know. This isn't where I thought we'd end up. Hmmm. I wonder where we are." She knit her brows and tried to look concerned.

"Maybe we better pull over and look at a map," Jeremy suggested.

"Good idea."

Jeremy coasted to a halt and stopped the car at the edge of the deserted overlook. Jessica looked out her window, trying to keep a smile off her face. Miller's Point was the famous—or infamous—parking spot widely used by students at Sweet Valley High.

You're bad, Jessica, tricking Jeremy into coming here. But desperate circumstances call for desperate measures. If only they had time alone, he would come to his senses and realize that he could never marry Sue. As much as Jessica liked her, anyone could see that she wasn't right for Jeremy. He needed someone more passionate, more mature. *Someone like me.*

Once they'd parked and rolled down their windows, a fresh, cool breeze off the ocean flooded the car.

"Hmmm. Smell that heavenly breeze," Jessica murmured, inhaling deeply.

"The air is so wonderful here—so fresh and clean. The air in Manhattan leaves something to be desired," Jeremy admitted. "Somehow it never feels as clean as the air does here."

On her side of the car, Jessica opened the glove compartment and searched for a map. She pulled it out and spread it clumsily across her lap.

"Jessica?"

She looked up. *There it is again, that longing and uncertainty in his eyes. But I'm not going to make this easy for him—any more than he's made it easy for me.* She looked down at the map again. He had to realize that they were meant to be together, but he had to realize it on his own. She wasn't going to give him cause to say that she had clouded his judgment or trapped him in any way.

"I think we need to go back down that hill," she said calmly, tracing her finger along a line on the map. Inside, her heart was pounding and her breath was coming fast and shallow.

As he leaned over to see where she was pointing, their heads almost touched.

"There's the problem. We turned left that first time instead of turning right." Jessica sat back and busily began to refold the map. "Now I know where we are. We need to—"

"Jessica." It was a plea.

Her hands stilled, and Jessica slowly turned to look into Jeremy's dark, dark eyes.

"What?" she whispered.

He leaned closer and gently brushed his lips against hers. *Finally,* she thought as exultation traveled through her spine. But she remained icily still. Only when he pulled away did she brush her mouth against his in a butterfly's touch. Jeremy jerked back as if burned.

"This is crazy," he said, his voice tight. He turned, staring out his own window.

"Yes, it is," Jessica said with a catch in her throat.

"Jessica, when you look at me like that—" he broke off and turned away again. "I'm engaged to marry Sue," he said firmly, but his voice wavered.

"Just start the car. They're waiting for us." Jessica was trembling with anger at his obstinance—and with longing for the love he was so cruelly withholding. Maybe sharing a kiss was wrong, but it sure felt right. Why couldn't he admit that?

"I just don't understand—" he began.

"Start the car, Jeremy. There's nothing to understand. Let's just go." Jessica felt near tears.

Jeremy started the car, and Jessica bit out terse directions that took them straight to Michael's catering.

"Hi, darling!" Sue cried, rushing over to Jeremy and throwing her arms around him. "What happened—did you get lost?"

Jessica turned away as Sue kissed him.

"I thought Mom was supposed to bring Jeremy," Elizabeth said, examining Jessica's face.

"She had an emergency meeting," Jessica explained. "She asked me to come."

Elizabeth raised her eyebrows.

"OK, are we all here now?" Mr. Robert, one of Michael's event planners, clapped his hands for attention. "I know you're all busy, so let's get started. May I have the bride and groom here?" He gestured to two small white chairs in front of his desk.

Taking Jeremy's hand, Sue led him over to the chairs.

"We'll be over here," Elizabeth told them, gesturing at the waiting area. There were various catalogues and photo albums of different events Michael's had catered.

When Jessica sat down on the couch next to

her, Elizabeth whispered, "So what happened to you? You and Jeremy both look as though you just saw a UFO."

"That's it. We both *did* just see a UFO. They wanted to kidnap us for scientific experiments, but we resisted."

Elizabeth giggled. "You're crazy. Now, what really happened? I thought we would lose our appointment with Mr. Robert."

Jessica looked away. "We took a wrong turn. I forgot how to get here."

"Liar," Elizabeth said calmly.

"Darling, don't you think the lobster would be better?" Sue's voice rose above the girls' conversation.

"Honey, that would cost a fortune. We would have to cut the guest list. But if we have the chicken, we can still have everyone you want to invite."

"But the invitations are going out tomorrow! I can't cut the guest list now. Besides, I've already told everyone."

Jeremy frowned impatiently. "Then I can't afford the lobster. Not if you want to have the champagne, too."

Sue looked horrified. "What's a wedding without champagne?"

"A lot of our guests won't even be old enough to drink," Jeremy reminded her. "*You're* even underage.

"Well, a wedding just isn't a wedding without champagne," Sue said firmly.

"I thought a wedding was supposed to be where we vow our love to each other forever, in front of our family and friends," Jeremy said dryly. "I wasn't aware that champagne was required to do that."

"Of course it is," Sue snapped.

Jessica saw a muscle in Jeremy's jaw start to twitch.

"Children, children," Mr. Robert intervened. "I see this all the time. It's simply nerves about the wedding, my dears. Why don't you take a moment to compose yourselves. I'll write down what we've agreed upon so far and wait for you here. Go on, now." He shooed them away briskly as he began to fill in his order form.

Jeremy and Sue, looking embarrassed, got up and walked over to a vending machine, where Jeremy bought a soda. They took turns sipping it, not looking at each other.

Elizabeth gave Jessica an accusing glance. "See what you've done!"

"What? Me? Are you nuts? I was sitting right here—I didn't do anything," Jessica whispered defensively.

"You've done something to Jeremy. He's arguing over everything," Elizabeth pointed out.

Wide-eyed, Jessica turned to her sister. "Elizabeth," she hissed, "has it occurred to you that maybe he's arguing because Sue wants all kinds of fancy stuff that costs too much money? He *is* the one paying for all this, so he should have a pretty good idea of what he can and can't afford. But that doesn't seem to make any difference to Sue."

Elizabeth sat silently for a moment. "OK, maybe you're right," she said finally. "I guess they just have different ideas of what they want for the wedding. It was the same way at the beach this morning. Sue made it clear that if it were up to her, she'd have the ceremony at the big church downtown, and the reception at the country club."

"Jeremy wants to keep it simple, and Sue wants it to be really fancy," Jessica concluded. "I can't really blame her—it's her only wedding, and of course she wants it to be nice."

"But they have to learn to compromise," Elizabeth agreed.

Over on the other side of the room, Jeremy and Sue started chuckling together. They threw away the empty can of soda and hugged each other. Once again, a brilliant smile lit Sue's face, and she practically skipped back over to Mr. Robert.

"OK," she told him. "We're having the champagne—with the chicken kiev."

"Excellent," said Mr. Robert, writing quickly.

Their voices lowered again as they discussed hors d'oeuvres, side dishes, and the wedding cake.

Sighing, Elizabeth turned to Jessica. "Now that's love," she said, starry-eyed. "Compromise, working together, each wanting the other one to be happy . . . it's so wonderful."

"Shut up," Jessica growled.

"Great idea, Jessica. All that talk about food has made me totally starving," Sue joked as they met in the parking lot of the Dairi Burger. She and Jeremy had gone in his rental car, and Elizabeth and Jessica had ridden in their black Jeep.

"Hey, you guys!" Lila called from the large booth she shared with Robby.

"Come on, this'll hold everybody," Robby invited. "I'll just have to snuggle up closer to Lila." He winked and everyone laughed.

They all crammed into the booth and ordered their hamburgers and fries. Jessica sat between Sue and Lila.

Robby and Jeremy were talking about college friends of theirs with whom Robby had kept in touch, and Sue started filling Lila in on the menu planned for the reception.

In the midst of the happy, chattering couples, Elizabeth met Jessica's gaze with a rueful look. Jessica understood immediately. Here were the popular, beautiful Wakefield twins, whom everyone envied, and they were about as welcome as fifth wheels in this booth at the Dairi Burger.

What had gone wrong with their love lives? Jessica saw her lonely, single future completely mapped out. There would be no life partner to share her milestones with—college, her twenty-first birthday, her first real job. . . . No one to help her celebrate the good times, to help her through

130

the bad times. It would always be Jessica, just Jessica.

Then Jessica felt a hand patting her own: Elizabeth's. Jessica didn't need to tell her what she was feeling—she already knew. And Jessica realized then that no matter if she was married or single, happy or sad, she wouldn't have to go through life alone, after all.

"Jessica? Jessica! Take your shake," Lila commanded, pushing the strawberry milk shake over to her.

"Oh, thanks." Jessica pulled it over and took a long, satisfying sip. Reaching for her plate of french fries, she licked off her strawberry milk mustache. When she looked up again, Jeremy was staring at her mouth. *Oh, get over it—like you're forcing me to do.* Jessica rolled her eyes to herself and looked down again.

"So, can we go shopping tomorrow for your bridesmaid dresses?" Sue was asking the twins excitedly.

"Uh-huh. I'm busy tomorrow night, but anytime during the day is fine for me," Elizabeth agreed, taking a french fry.

"Just tell me when," Jessica said, trying to sound at least a smidgin enthusiastic.

"Great. They've been so wonderful," Sue gushed to Lila. "Without Elizabeth and Jessica, this wedding might never take place!" She gazed adoringly into Jeremy's eyes. He quickly turned to smile at her.

"Good old Jessica," Lila said, smirking at her. "What a pal."

131

"Oh, my goodness, Jessica—don't look now," Sue said, putting her hand over her mouth.

Jessica immediately turned to look.

"What?" she asked, confused. She hadn't seen anything that would cause Sue to have that reaction—it was just Bruce and Pamela, coming into the Dairi . . .

"Oh," Jessica said. Then she deliberately looked brave and unconcerned. "Don't worry, Sue. I'm sure it's nothing."

Turning again, Jessica saw Bruce pull out Pamela's chair, then lean down to kiss her on the lips before he sat down himself.

Casually eating a french fry, Jessica felt a perverse sense of pleasure. "They're just good friends. He told me so." She pasted an artificial smile on her face and turned to talk to Lila, who was practically eating her napkin. *Real effective way to keep yourself from laughing, Lila,* Jessica thought.

"That guy needs to be taught a lesson," Jeremy ground out, glaring at Bruce.

"Uh, no, Jeremy—don't worry about it. It's fine," Jessica insisted, remembering how weird Jeremy had been about Bruce.

"The nerve of him," Jeremy continued, getting visibly angrier by the second. "You deserve better than that, Jessica."

Jessica felt something snap inside her. "You're right, Jeremy," she said coldly. "I deserve someone who will love me and *only* me. Every woman deserves that—Sue, Lila, Elizabeth. But I hardly think that *you* are the person to teach Bruce that lesson." Her breath was coming hard and fast.

Jeremy's face paled as though he'd been hit over the head. Then he flushed an angry red. "Fine. You're right," he muttered.

Sue looked from Jessica to Jeremy, a completely bewildered expression on her face.

Chapter 11

"Get up, sleepyhead," Elizabeth said way too perkily after slapping Jessica's rump on Friday morning. "Let's get this show on the road. We have to go get our bridesmaid dresses today."

Opening one eye, Jessica peered up at Elizabeth's no-nonsense face. "You're awfully military this morning," she mumbled.

"I'm just taking charge of my own life, that's all." She checked her watch. "I'm leaving for the mall with Sue in exactly forty-five minutes. If you're dressed by then, fine. If not, you'll have to accept whatever bridesmaid dress I pick out. The ball's in your court." She gave Jessica a cheerful smile and bounced out of the room.

Jessica turned over on her other side and snuggled into the covers. Elizabeth would give her two more warnings before pretending to leave without her. No problem.

Then she opened her eyes again. Elizabeth *had* been a little different lately. For one thing, she had been hardly meddling in Jessica's affairs at all. Usually she could be counted on to spend at least some of her time worrying about Jessica's latest scrape. But she had been so caught up in this sisterhood-empowerment thing that Jessica's problems had taken a backseat. It was almost disconcerting.

Taking charge of her own life, Jessica thought. Maybe there was something to that, after all. She hadn't been seizing the reins over the last week, that was for sure. The wedding was still taking place, as though Jessica didn't even exist.

Jessica sat up, throwing off the covers. No more sleeping and no more moping. No more wimpy plans like that trip to Miller's Point either—a lot *that* did to stop the wedding and make Jeremy admit to the world that *she* was the love of his life. So it was time for her to quit mooning around like a sick cow and to come up with one of her daring, risky, surefire Jessica schemes.

"With your coloring," Sue mused, "you can really wear almost any shade of fabric." She, Jessica, and Elizabeth were back in Bridal Glory, looking for bridesmaid dresses.

Elizabeth nodded. "Have you decided on a color theme for the wedding?"

"I was thinking peach, green, and gold," Sue told her. "My bouquet will be peach-colored roses, and we'll probably have a couple of large flower arrangements around the serving area of the beach tent. That reminds me—we need to go to the florist sometime soon." Frowning, Sue took her wedding-planner book out of her shoulder bag and quickly scribbled some notes.

"Those colors sound pretty. Don't you think so, Jess?"

"Sure, whatever," Jessica said, examining wedding dresses. Taking one off its rack, she held it up in front of her and looked in the full-length mirror. "What do you think of this?" she asked her sister.

"Jessica!" Sue laughed. "Are you planning on getting married soon, too?"

Jessica gave her a cryptic smile in the mirror. "You never know," she said airily.

"Well, right now we need to find bridesmaid dresses that we can all agree on," Elizabeth reminded her. "Have you seen anything you like?"

Jessica shrugged. "Not really."

"Well, let's look over here." Elizabeth took the wedding dress out of Jessica's hands and led her over to several racks of bridesmaid dresses. "What about this one?" she asked, holding up a sea-green, floaty dress. "Sue?"

Sue looked at it carefully. It had thin spaghetti straps, a fitted bodice, and a full skirt of several layers of chiffon.

"Hmmm. I'm not sure. It's pretty, but . . ."

Elizabeth put it back. Riffling through the racks, she found a pretty, dark peach dress that had wide, ruffled short sleeves and was almost backless. It looked cool and summery.

"What do you think of this?" she asked Sue.

Sue's brown eyes lit up. "That's really pretty. I like it. What about you?"

Looking at the dress, Elizabeth nodded. "Yeah. I think it's pretty, and the style would be easy to wear again. Most bridesmaid dresses are worn once, and then they just hang around in someone's closet forever."

"What do you think, Jessica? Elizabeth and I both like this one."

"Ewww." Jessica looked up from a rack of dresses and wrinkled her nose. "It looks so babyish. But look what I found." She held up a strapless, form-fitted gold lamé dress with glittery bugle-bead trim. The skirt was so short that it looked as though the bottom half was missing. "What do you think? With gold high heels?"

Elizabeth looked at her in exasperation. "I think it would be great—if we were dealing blackjack in Vegas. Come on now, Jess. Get serious. We have to decide."

Pouting, Jessica hung her dress on the nearest rack.

"Hey—this is it!" Sue had been looking at some dresses on an adjoining rack, and now she held up an elegant, drop-waisted, pale peach sheath, similar in style to her own wedding dress, but without any lace, and falling just below the knee.

"I love it," Elizabeth exclaimed, going over and taking it from Sue. Standing in front of the long mirror, she held it against herself. "It's gorgeous, Sue. Are you sure it's dressy enough?"

Squinting her eyes critically, Sue nodded. "I think so. I like the fact that it's similar to mine, and with your hair piled on your head, and some dressy peach pumps—I think you'll be beautiful."

"Well, I would love to have it. I can think of a dozen places I can wear it to after the wedding. Todd will love me in it."

"I'm sure Todd would love you no matter what you were wearing," Sue said loyally. "What about you, Jessica? Is the dress OK with you?"

"No," Jessica said flatly. "I think it looks like a rag. And I think—"

"Excuse us a minute, Sue," Elizabeth said firmly, grabbing Jessica's arm and hauling her away. "We'll be back in a flash," she added over her shoulder.

Over by the fitting rooms, where they were out of Sue's earshot, Elizabeth hissed, "What's the matter with you? This dress is perfect, and you know it!"

"I don't like it," Jessica said diffidently.

139

"You just don't like it because it's not white," Elizabeth accused.

"So what? This whole wedding is a farce," Jessica shot back. "I refuse to be party to it. You know as well as I do that it should never take place, and—"

"Jessica Wakefield," Elizabeth began, bringing her face right up to Jessica's, "you are going to wear this dress and be a bridesmaid for this wedding, and you are going to behave yourself during it, or so help me . . ."

"So help you what?" Jessica challenged. She had never seen Elizabeth like this, and it was interesting.

"Or I'll . . . I'll . . . I'll convince Sue the *really* romantic thing to do would be to elope!" Elizabeth finished triumphantly.

Jessica went pale. "You wouldn't."

"I most certainly would. I would convince Sue, and she would convince Jeremy, who I think would *jump* at the idea, since he doesn't want all this fuss anyway. Now, you can either wear this dress and be a good sport, or you can continue to be a pill and have Sue and Jeremy gone out of our lives for good. You decide."

With that, Elizabeth stomped back to Sue, who was trying on assorted pairs of silk shoes.

All this empowerment stuff is turning Liz into a real witch, Jessica thought grumpily. She decided that the upper hand didn't become

Elizabeth at all. Sighing, Jessica made her way through the racks of dresses, then pasted a sweet smile on her face.

"This dress is great," she said cheerfully. "Do they have two of them, in size six?"

"Here, I'll carry your dress for you, Sue. You look pretty loaded down," Jessica offered as they headed out to the parking lot after lunchtime. After Sue had bought heaps of bridal accessories, they had picked up her dress, which had needed only a few alterations.

Sue gave Jessica the dress and tapped her bag full of bridal underthings. "After all, I want to feel special from head to foot on our wedding day," Sue said. "I hope Jeremy likes them!" She blushed and giggled nervously.

Jessica spun to look at her in shock. Jeremy *would* see Sue in her underwear—after the wedding. This was unbearable. *How can I just let this happen?* Feeling sick and dizzy, Jessica lagged behind the other girls. A pickup truck crossed her path, and almost without thinking about what she was doing, she threw Sue's wedding dress right under the truck's huge, mud-track wheels. With a giddy mixture of shame, guilt, and pleasure, she watched the truck roll over the dress, then screech to a halt as the driver realized what had happened.

"Oh, no!" Jessica managed a perfectly genuine gasp of shock. Turning around, Sue and Elizabeth both shrieked as they saw the plastic garment bag containing Sue's dress under the truck's wheels.

"My dress!" Sue screamed. "My wedding dress! Oh, my God! What happened? Jessica, what have you done to my dress! My wedding dress!"

"Do you think maybe some spot remover?" Jessica asked her mother, trying to sound hopeful.

Sue's poor wedding dress was spread out carefully on the Wakefields' dining-room table, and Mrs. Wakefield was examining the fabric.

"Jessica, this was unbelievably careless of you. Sue's beautiful, expensive dress . . . it could have been completely destroyed," Alice Wakefield said firmly.

"What do you mean—*could have* been?" Jessica asked.

"You mean, it's not destroyed?" Sue asked, her voice quavering. After the truck driver had jumped out, protesting that he didn't know what had happened, they had gathered the dress together and taken it to the Wakefields'. Sue had cradled it in her arms, weeping all the way home. Elizabeth had been tight-lipped and curt, sending Jessica withering glances in the rearview mirror. Jessica had kept her hand over her mouth so that she wouldn't grin. This little mishap was sure at least to delay the wedding.

142

"No, it isn't," the twins' mother confirmed. "The fabric isn't actually ripped or ruined anywhere. You're lucky that you chose a relatively simple style, with no beads or heavy embroidery, Sue. I know of a special French dry cleaners that specializes in irreplaceable gowns. I think they'll be able to clean the dress and make it look perfect again. Of course, they're very expensive. But Jessica will be happy to pay the bill."

"What?" Jessica cried.

Her mother turned a stern look on her. "If the dress had been destroyed, you would have somehow paid for a new one, Jessica. I think you're getting off lightly. Now, I want you to take this dress to Pierre Marchand's, over on Holly Drive. And if anything else happens to it, I can guarantee that you won't get an allowance for the rest of your natural life."

Jessica stared at her mother in horror. It would cost a fortune to special-clean a wedding dress! And this was on top of paying for Bruce to stuff his face at the Carousel! Setting her jaw, Jessica picked up the dress and stormed out of the house.

Elizabeth tapped on Jessica's door. When no one answered, she went in to find her twin face-down on her bed, kicking her heels aimlessly in the air. No doubt about it, Jessica was sulking big-time. Privately Elizabeth thought Jessica had gotten off easily. It was all too clear to Elizabeth what had

143

happened, though neither Sue nor their mother seemed to suspect it had been anything more than gross negligence.

"Are you OK? You hardly ate any dinner." Stepping over some laundry and magazines, Elizabeth came to sit next to Jessica on the bed.

"I'm just fine," Jessica said sarcastically.

"I'm not going to discuss the wedding with you," Elizabeth said firmly. "I only came in to see if you wanted to do something with me tonight. That is, if you're not seeing Bruce." Elizabeth smiled mischievously.

"Oh, ha ha," Jessica grumbled.

"No, seriously—Sue is already gone. She and Jeremy went to the mall to register for their wedding presents. So it's just you and me. And I know something fun we could do that would take your mind off of everything."

"Really?" Jessica asked.

"OK, sisters, everyone sit in a circle!"

"I don't believe this," Jessica groaned. "I do not believe this."

"Come on and sit down," Elizabeth instructed, pulling Jessica down beside her on the floor of the Sweet Valley Community Center. She hoped that once they got started, Jessica would find a lot of value in the theory of female empowerment. For one thing, maybe it would help her stop chasing a man who was practically already married.

"Hello, and welcome to Sweet Valley's first *Primal Woman* seminar," the woman who seemed to be in charge said. Everyone in the large circle on the floor cheered and whistled. "My name is Sharon Wilson, and I'm your group leader tonight. This seminar is based on the book *Primal Woman, Woman of Strength*, by Mary Beth Hudson. Some of you may have read it."

Several women clapped and nodded.

"Tonight we're going to explore our inner selves—the selves inside of us that are kept hidden because they're strong, they're powerful, they're dynamic—and therefore they're considered unfeminine and threatening to men."

More women cheered and clapped.

"And now, let's begin!" Sharon said.

Jessica dropped her face into her hands, and Elizabeth nudged her sharply with her elbows.

"This is totally asinine," Jessica hissed under her breath, "even for you."

Elizabeth giggled. "Your animal fur is slipping, Jess," she whispered.

When they had arrived at the community center, they had each been given a little cape of fake fur. Elizabeth's was gray, and Jessica's was spotted like a leopard. Now they and about twenty-five other women of all ages were seated in a large circle on the linoleum floor. In the center of the circle was a small hibachi.

"Traditionally, our sisters of ancient time would

145

gather like this around a fire in the middle of their community," their group leader said. "Of course, as we're indoors, we can't light our fire, but the hibachi is here as a symbol."

Elizabeth could feel Jessica's unbelieving eyes boring a hole in her head, but she steadfastly ignored her. Soon Jessica would be as caught up in the exciting spirit as Elizabeth was, and then she would see what she had been missing.

"We've assembled here together tonight to seize our heritage as women," Sharon cried. "We're going to block out thousands of years of *his*tory, and replace it with our own *her*story. We are women, we are the strength of the earth, we are an unstoppable force!"

Elizabeth cheered along with the others, and nudged Jessica again. "Yay," Jessica said, rolling her eyes.

"Now," Sharon said, "let's see who we are. You—" She pointed right at Jessica. "What's your name?"

"Jessica Wakefield."

Sharon looked around the circle. "Sisters, every one of us here carries either our husband's last name or our father's. Women in our society are not allowed to have their *own* last names. Names are not passed down from mother to daughter, but from father to daughter. But that time is over! Let us now choose our own names for this circle. Let us reclaim that right. Jessica Wakefield!"

146

"Me?" Jessica squeaked.

"Yes, you. What name would you choose for yourself—a name that is no man's, but solely your own," Sharon said in her strong, regal voice. Her black eyes stared at Jessica.

Elizabeth felt a thrill of excitement. *A name solely my own.* What name would she choose? She had never minded Elizabeth Wakefield, but this was her chance to start over, to be someone else, someone more powerful, more independent. . . .

"How about just plain Jessica?" Jessica suggested. "You know, like Cher, or Sade, or Madonna. I would be just—Jessica."

Sharon seemed to give up on Jessica, at least momentarily, and turned to the person on Jessica's other side.

"I choose the name Shakara," the woman said. She was a mousy blonde in her thirties.

"Shakara," Sharon repeated approvingly. "That's a real name, a warrior's name."

"And what's *Jessica?* Chopped liver?" Jessica whispered angrily to Elizabeth.

"Shhh," Elizabeth whispered back, as Sharon moved around the circle.

The next woman, a sweet-faced, grandmotherly type, said her new name was Lion-Woman.

"Fabulous!" Sharon gushed. "That's fabulous."

By the time they got to Elizabeth, she had decided. "My name is Runs-with-the-Wind." That was the name that really summed up the feelings she wanted to express.

"Wonderful. That's a wonderful name," Sharon said approvingly. "Now, we need to break down some more of the shackles that our male-dominated society has put on us. One of our strongest fears is the fear of being thought unfeminine. That fear keeps us from doing many things we want to do, and many things we ought to do."

The women in the circle nodded and murmured their agreement.

Sharon continued, "One of the characteristics considered unfeminine is loudness, noisiness. Women are supposed to be soft-spoken, mild, agreeable, quiet, gentle, docile, etc. The exercise I would like us to do now to break that mold is for us to make a lot of NOISE." A thrill went down Elizabeth's spine as Sharon practically shouted the last word.

"Now, women, let's stand up, and I want each of you to let out a real, womanly, powerful yell. I want you to reach deep into your primal gut and really pour out some deep-seated emotion. Don't be afraid of being loud. There's no one here but us. Shakara, would you begin?"

The woman to Jessica's left stood up, and after a few moments of uncertainty let out a medium-sized yelp.

"Good start, Shakara," Sharon said. "Now that you've broken the ice, your sisters may find it easier. Fire-Maker?" A woman sitting on the other side of the circle stood, then clenched her fists, screwed up her face, and screamed.

Jessica leaned close to Elizabeth and spoke out of the side of her mouth. "I can't even think of what you're going to have to do to make this up to me," she whispered.

"Oh, be quiet," Elizabeth said crossly. "I was doing you a favor by getting you out of the house."

One by one the women stood up to yell, and Elizabeth found herself looking forward to her turn. Finally, after Flower-in-the-Sun, Lion-Woman, and Kolanda had yelled, Sharon said, "Runs-with-the-Wind?"

Elizabeth stood up and summoned every ounce of lung power she had. She thought of all the times she had wanted to raise her voice in an argument, but hadn't, because she hadn't wanted to anger her friends, or Todd, or her parents, or Jessica. She thought of all the times she had played peace-maker when she really wanted just to tell people to shut up and grow up. She thought of the time she had seen her favorite movie star on the street, but hadn't screamed because it seemed so juvenile. Then she opened her mouth, took a deep breath, and let it all out.

It seemed to take minutes, and when she fin-ished, she was hoarse and almost lightheaded. Sitting down again at her spot in the circle, she was aware of Jessica's wide-eyed face staring at her.

149

Blushing, she looked around, and saw that all the women of her circle were gazing at her with surprise and admiration.

"Now, that's what I call a *Primal Woman* shout," Sharon said, smiling and nodding at Elizabeth. "I could really feel the ancient force of the earth mother rising through your voice. Sisters, let's all give Runs-With-the-Wind a big hand."

Elizabeth blushed deeper as the circle applauded her.

"You ought to change your name to Hurricane-Lungs," Jessica told Elizabeth as they drove home in their Jeep after the meeting.

"And you ought to be called Squeaks-Like-a-Mouse, you sissy," Elizabeth derided her. "Honestly, Jessica, you weren't even trying."

"It just wasn't me," Jessica said. "As I was about to scream, I just thought: what if there were boys outside, spying on us? They would die laughing."

"Jessica, the whole point is to quit living your life according to what boys might think. The point is just to be yourself, your true, womanly self."

"Hmm. Well, I think my true womanly self happens to care about what boys think. I can't help it. It's my nature."

Elizabeth groaned as she turned onto Calico Drive. "I take it back. Your name ought to be She-Who-Primps-a-Lot." She giggled.

Jessica swatted Elizabeth's arm. "Oh, stop it."

"How about Shops-at-the-Mall?"

"No, I know—I'll call myself Stylesetter-Woman," Jessica suggested.

"Perfect," Elizabeth agreed, heading for their driveway. "Next time you renew your library card, make sure they put Stylesetter-Woman on it."

Chapter 12

"Jessica! What are you doing up so early? I think this is a Saturday-morning record for you," Mrs. Wakefield said cheerfully.

"Couldn't sleep," Jessica muttered. "Kept having awful dreams about being a cavewoman. I was running around with a huge club, trying to catch a saber-tooth squirrel for dinner."

Elizabeth giggled. "Were you named Squirrel-Slayer?"

Jessica turned around from where she was putting some frozen waffles into the toaster and grinned at her sister. "Did you tell everyone about our wild-woman experience last night?"

"She was just finishing up," Sue said. "It sounds so interesting. I wish I could have gone. Maybe next time."

"Did you and Jeremy get everything done at

the mall last night?" Elizabeth asked her.

Jessica felt a sting at the sound of his name. She studied the toaster oven so that no one could see the flush rising in her cheeks. Time was running out. . . . Why couldn't she come up with a great plan to make Jeremy see the light?

"Um, pretty much," Sue said. "We registered for crystal and china at Lytton & Brown, and picked out our silverware at the mall branch of Tiffany's."

"Wow, I hope you can fit all that in your backpacks as you tramp around South America," Jessica said casually, sitting down and putting syrup on her waffles.

Sue smiled. "You sound like Jeremy. He couldn't see the point of having nice china and serving dishes. But I think every bride wants those things."

"I'm sure he'll be glad to have them when you two have your first dinner party," Mrs. Wakefield said.

Sue's young face looked troubled. "I hope so. He really didn't enjoy looking at everything last night. He's acting so cool and distant. And sometimes I felt like he was disagreeing with me just to disagree. If I wanted one china pattern, he wanted something else. He didn't want crystal at all. And he said the silverware I wanted was absolutely tacky!" For a moment Sue looked near tears.

Elizabeth reached over and patted Sue's arm reassuringly.

Jessica felt her heart fill with hope. Maybe Jeremy was coming to his senses after all. Maybe he was seeing it wasn't Sue he wanted to have dinner parties with.

"Now, dear, don't worry about it for a moment," her mother said with too much conviction. "Jeremy is behaving perfectly normally for an engaged man. It's called cold feet, and everyone gets them before the wedding. He probably just feels nervous about taking such a big step, and it's showing up in all these little ways. Just try to remember that, and not blame him too much."

Sue's face looked more cheerful, and she nodded, saying, "You know, Aunt Alice, I bet you're right. As soon as the wedding plans are all settled, he'll be his old self again." She smiled gratefully at Mrs. Wakefield. "Thanks. I'm sure that's what my mom would have told me, if she could be here." For a moment her smile wavered, and she looked away.

Frowning, Jessica finished up her waffles. *Mom, maybe you should just stay out of it.*

"So, what are our plans for today?" Elizabeth asked.

Sue opened her wedding planner, which accompanied her everywhere lately. "Today I wanted to double check the beach location, then get information about what permits we'll need. Then we should go to the florist and start pricing bouquets and decorations for the tent." She glanced up at

155

the kitchen clock and frowned. "Jeremy was supposed to call by now. He wanted to join us for all this stuff."

"Well, I'm free this morning, so I'll be happy to come with you," Mrs. Wakefield said.

"Me too," said Elizabeth.

Sue looked expectantly at Jessica.

"Uh—well, first I have to go pick up Sue's dress. It should be ready this morning. Then I think I might stay here and do some laundry," Jessica said, trying to think fast. She simply couldn't bear another wedding-planning expedition with Sunny Sue. She'd rather mope at home. "Maybe I'll clean my room or something."

"What have you done with the real Jessica?" her mother demanded, in mock alarm.

Jessica smiled cynically. "Thanks for your vote of confidence," she said dryly.

Just then the phone rang, and Elizabeth jumped up to get it.

"Hello? Hi, Jeremy. We were just talking about you. Hold on a minute—Sue's right here." She handed to phone to Sue.

"Hello? Yeah. Me too. Oh, thanks, sweetie, that's really nice. You do? Good, I do too. Uh-huh. Yeah, the beach first. In a few minutes. Oh, no—really? When? OK—about an hour, then? OK. Great. OK, see you. Love you too."

When Sue hung up the phone, her face had its customary Jeremy-glow and her eyes were shining.

"Jeremy's running a little late—he's helping Robby change the oil in his car or some manly thing like that. He's going to call back in an hour."

"Oh, that's no problem. You guys go on," Jessica said immediately, ignoring Elizabeth's suspicious gaze. "I'll be back from the dry cleaners soon, and when Jeremy calls back I'll tell him to meet you at the florist's."

"OK, but for heaven's sake, don't give him directions," Mrs. Wakefield said, putting her dishes in the dishwasher. She had heard all about the getting-lost-on-the-way-to-the-caterers episode.

Sue giggled, then came and gave Jessica a quick hug. "Poor Jessica! Everyone's picking on you. But I know you're doing your best."

Jessica smiled weakly.

Sue's wedding dress was indeed ready, and Pierre Marchand proudly pointed out all the places he had had to clean it by hand. To Jessica's disappointment, it did look perfect. And perfection didn't come cheap. Gnashing her teeth, Jessica paid the ninety-five-dollar bill. Then she hung the dress carefully in the Jeep and drove home.

Jessica did some laundry as she waited for Jeremy's call. When the phone finally rang, she practically fell over the mountainous dry-clean-only pile as she ran to answer it.

Her heart beat when she heard his voice. "Sue asked me to tell you to come by here when you were ready," she said. "They should be done at the beach soon, and she thought you could go to the florist together."

"Really? She must have changed her plans since I spoke to her this morning," Jeremy said.

"I guess," Jessica said, sounding bored.

"OK. I'll be by in a while. Thanks."

"Sure."

After they had hung up, Jessica ran around in excited circles for a moment. What a fabulous opportunity! She hadn't had a chance to be alone with Jeremy since that awful day at the caterer's. Now, on top of his and Sue's squabbling at the store the night before, she had this golden opportunity to see him and carry out her brilliant plan.

Except that she didn't exactly have a brilliant plan. Nothing. Nada. Zip. She would simply have to improvise when Jeremy showed up. What should she be doing? What should she be wearing?

Maybe she should be folding her laundry—looking domestic. Jessica thought of what Sharon Wilson, her *Primal Woman* seminar leader, would say to that.

Maybe she should be in her new black bikini, lounging by the pool. But that might be a bit much. And he had already seen her in a bathing suit—twice.

158

She could be washing the Jeep—with her shorts and T-shirt all wet and sudsy, who knew what might happen?

Jessica sighed. Subtle or obvious? Seductive or wholesome? Why couldn't she figure it out? She'd known how to act and be and look around the opposite sex since birth. Why was Jeremy so different? So difficult?

Because he's a man. He's not a boy, he's not a teenager, he's not even single. He's an older, engaged man, and he's dangerous.

The doorbell punctuated her thoughts. Breathlessly Jessica ran to the door and opened it. Jeremy stood before her, looking taller and broader and handsomer than ever. His eyes darkened when he saw her.

"Hi," she said softly, standing aside to let him in.

"Hi," he returned with a slight rasp in his voice. "Is Sue here?"

"Oh, no. She called right after I spoke to you and said she was running a little late. But she should probably be here soon," Jessica lied. "Why don't you wait for her?"

"Oh. OK." Jeremy looked hesitant, then followed Jessica to the den.

"What's that you're carrying?" Jessica asked, motioning to the garment bag over his arm.

"It's my tux. For the wedding. I wanted to see if it went OK with Sue's dress. But I'll just check it another time."

159

"You don't have much time left," Jessica commented, the wheels whirling in her head. "In fact, why don't you go ahead and put on your tux. Sue will be here any second. The powder room's through there."

Turning, Jessica ran down the hall and up the stairs, her heart racing as she ran into Sue's room and started throwing off her clothes.

Ten minutes later she started to descend the steps to the first floor. She heard footsteps, and Jeremy came to stand at the bottom of the staircase. *Oh, my gosh, he's even more gorgeous in a tux. If that's possible,* Jessica thought. His dark eyes were burning as he gazed at her in the beautiful white dress, a headpiece of tiny white roses nestled on her shining blond hair. His mouth dropped open slightly, and Jessica flushed under his intense gaze.

When she reached the bottom of the staircase, Jessica glided to the long hall mirror in the entranceway, her bare feet making only the faintest sound against the floor. Just as silently, Jeremy came to stand beside her, and his strong brown hands reached out to grip her shoulders.

They stared at their reflection in the hall mirror. They looked just like a young, beautiful, happy bride and groom.

"Your tux," she said huskily, "looks really nice with the dress."

Jeremy nodded, still staring at their image in

the mirror. "You're a beautiful bride," he whispered hoarsely. "The most beautiful bride I've ever seen."

"I'm not a bride, Jeremy," Jessica said. "Remember?"

"I wish—" Jeremy said, then broke off.

"You wish what?"

"Nothing." Taking a careful step back, Jeremy dropped his hands from her shoulders and looked away.

Jessica whirled to face him. "I'll tell you what *I* wish—that it was me you were marrying! How can you go through with it, Jeremy? You know you love me, not Sue!"

"No, Jessica—you don't know what you're saying—"

"I do so. And you know it's true. You knew it the moment we met on the beach." Jessica stepped closer to him, looking up at him with her wide blue-green eyes.

"Jessica." Jeremy reached up to hold her shoulders again.

"You know you love me," Jessica said with certainty, putting her hands on his chest.

"No—I don't know." Jeremy frowned. "Sue—"

Jessica stood up on her bare tiptoes and brought her face close to Jeremy's. Softly, slowly, deliberately she pressed her lips against his. Time seemed to stop. They were together at last, touching as they had that day on the beach.

Except that now Jeremy stood perfectly still. The arms that should have circled her waist and pressed her close stayed at his sides. He wasn't kissing her back. He didn't want her.

You're such a fool, you never know when to quit. Gasping, she turned and ran into the den, where she threw herself on the couch. The tears she had been fighting for days finally came flowing out. She had to stop acting like this. She would become more like Elizabeth. Except Elizabeth had gotten hurt too, recently. Love was the most miserable, horrible, poisonous. . .

"Honey, honey, please don't cry. Jessica, sweetie . . ."

Then his hands were smoothing the dress against her shoulders and running down her arms, and his fingers entwined with hers.

"Go away," she sniffled. "I'm sorry I embarrassed you. I won't do it again." Her heart was breaking; she wanted to die.

"Jessica, you didn't embarrass me. Come on, now, stop crying, sweetie."

Jessica felt a tissue being pushed into her hand, and she took it, trying to stop sniffling. *He must think I'm a total baby.* In her whole sixteen years, she didn't think she had ever been so mortified.

Jeremy pulled her gently forward until he could circle his arms around her. He began cuddling her on the couch.

162

Jessica gazed down at the rumpled tissue in her hand, unable to look into his eyes.

"Jessica, I'm sorry. Please forgive me. It's all my fault." His voice was rich and deep and infinitely soothing.

"Forgive you for what?" Jessica asked in a small voice. *For being the love of my life who doesn't love me back?*

"Jessica—you're right. I do love you."

For a few moments Jessica forgot to breathe.

"I knew it the moment I saw you on the beach," Jeremy went on softly. "It was like we were connected somehow, like we had always known each other."

"Yes," Jessica breathed. Her head was spinning—she wasn't crazy after all. Jeremy *had* felt the same things she had felt.

"And now, every time I see you, it gets harder. . . . I hate seeing you, hate seeing how beautiful you are, how full of life. You reach out and grab life, Jessica. You're not afraid of anything—you don't let anything stop you. I never thought I would ever meet a woman like that."

"But you have," she said softly, her eyes shining.

Jeremy's fingers gently stroked Jessica's hair off her face. "But when we met," he continued, a frown marring his handsome features, "I was already engaged to Sue. We had been working together so much, and we just drifted into it. . . . It just seemed like a good idea at the time."

"But if you don't love her . . ."

"That's just it—I do love her. She's nice, and fun, and we have a lot in common. And—I don't know. She seems to need someone to take care of her."

"You love both of us?" Jessica asked, her eyes narrowing. She hadn't come this far to be one of a crowd.

"Not in the same way," Jeremy hastened to explain. "I love Sue more like a sister, or a good friend. And you I love . . ."

Jessica thought she would drown in his coffee-dark eyes. Then his head was bending toward hers, and she held her breath. But he pulled back again, shaking his head as though to clear it. "Well, I love you in a different way. Not very brotherly," he clarified, grimacing.

"So what does all this mean? What's going to become of us?" Sighing, Jeremy sat back and moved away a little. He raked a hand through his honey-blond hair, making it stand up in tangled waves. "That's just it. Jessica, I've given my word to Sue. I've been tearing myself up, thinking about it, but I just can't see how I could break the engagement. It means too much to her. I'm the only really stable thing in her life, and she needs me."

"I need you too!" Jessica cried.

Jeremy shook his head. "You're beautiful, Jessica, and exciting and unpredictable—but

164

you're only sixteen. Not even out of high school yet. This might be only an infatuation for you. Besides," he said, smiling and running gentle fingers down her face, "you're much stronger than Sue is. You can handle yourself—you don't need anybody."

"I do so. I need you," Jessica repeated stubbornly.

He took her hand, and they sat quietly for a few moments.

"Where is Sue, really?" Jeremy said with a slight smile.

Jessica grinned sheepishly. "Waiting for you at the florist."

Laughing, Jeremy stood to leave. "I better go meet her, then."

"I don't understand how you can go through with this wedding," Jessica said, walking with him to the door. "Not when you love me and I love you."

"Jessica," Jeremy said regretfully, "you and I just met at the wrong time. If you were a few years older, or I was younger and hadn't met Sue . . . it all could have turned out differently. But I *am* engaged to Sue, and I can't break it. I have to keep my word. Do you understand?"

"No." Jessica turned luminous ocean-colored eyes to him.

"Well, OK, but you will soon—and you'll thank me for trying to keep my head. Please promise me you're going to try to forget about me, forget we ever had this talk."

"No."

"Please quit looking at me as though I've broken your heart."

"I think you have," Jessica whispered, feeling tears welling up again.

"No, Jessica," Jeremy said, giving her one last, brief hug. "Someday someone special is going to come along and knock your socks clean off, and he'll be a very lucky guy. But it isn't going to be me."

"I'm not wearing socks," Jessica pointed out sadly.

Jeremy laughed, and Jessica couldn't help smiling through her tears.

"Jessica, I have to go. But I'll be thinking of you and wishing things were different. Take care, honey," Jeremy said huskily, then he strode down the front walk toward his car.

Hateful dress, she thought, trudging upstairs to take it off once Jeremy had driven away. Once in her room, she reached around in back of herself and yanked the zipper down impatiently. The zipper stopped. Jessica reached around the other way, gripped the tab between her fingers, and pulled again. It went a fraction of an inch and stopped. Biting her lip, Jessica pulled it one last time, harder, felt it give a tiny bit, and then heard a sickening ripping sound. Then it stopped again. She was stuck.

"Jess? I'm home!" Elizabeth called, flinging

open the front door. Her mother and Sue had dropped her off so the groceries wouldn't melt while they went to fill Mrs. Wakefield's car with gas.

Elizabeth put the groceries away, expecting to hear the pattering sound of Jessica coming downstairs. She looked out the French doors to the patio, but Jessica wasn't out by the pool, either. The Jeep was out front; where could she be?

"Jessica? Are you here?" Elizabeth called as she headed upstairs. At the top of the stairs she saw the door to Jessica's room open a crack, and then Jessica's eye peeping through the small opening.

"Jess? What's the matter?"

"Are you alone?" Jessica hissed.

"Uh-huh. Mom and Sue should be here any minute, though. What's going—"

Jessica opened her door all the way, grabbed Elizabeth's arm, and hauled her inside.

Elizabeth gasped when she saw her sister. "Are you insane?" she screeched. "Take that dress off this minute!"

"I would if I could," Jessica said dryly, turning to show Elizabeth the stuck zipper.

"It's ripped!" Elizabeth said in horror. "Oh, Jessica, how could you? It's not enough that you threw it under the wheels of a truck—"

"I told you, it slipped out of my hands," Jessica responded testily. "Now will you please get this thing off me?"

167

"OK, OK, hold still," Elizabeth said, gently trying to work the zipper free of the fabric. "I don't even want to know what you're doing in this dress."

"Do you think you could mend the little rip?" Jessica asked hopefully.

"I guess so," Elizabeth said reluctantly. "How did you even get into it? It's too small for you. You feel like a stuffed sausage. Hold in your breath." She finally worked the zipper all the way down, and Jessica stepped out of the dress.

"It wasn't easy," Jessica admitted, hanging the dress on its padded hanger and smoothing it out. "But, Elizabeth, Jeremy was here, and he—"

"Oh, God, Jessica, not again," Elizabeth groaned. "Haven't you learned anything? Look, here in *Real Women, Bad Men* there's a whole section called 'Men You Can't Have.'" She took the book off Jessica's desk, where she had put it earlier in the hopes that Jessica would take its advice. She cleared her throat. "'Chasing a man you can't have is a symptom of feelings of deep-rooted inadequa—'"

"Will you give it a rest, Liz? That book doesn't know me, and it doesn't know Jeremy. It's just a bunch of nonsense!" Jessica seized the book from Elizabeth's hands, opened her door, and threw the fat paperback over the stairwell.

Seconds later they heard a loud *thunk!*, and then Sue's startled cry, "Ouch! Where did that come from?"

168

Eyes round with horror, Elizabeth and Jessica stared at each other. Then Elizabeth bolted out of Jessica's room and down the stairs. "Oh, Sue, I'm so sorry—the book just slipped out of my hands . . ."

Jessica pushed Sue's wedding dress to the back of her closet, then buried her face in her pillow to smother her hysterical, helpless giggles.

Chapter 13

"So what's Sue doing today?" Enid asked, bending down to dip her brush into the can of paint on Monday morning. She was redecorating her room, and Elizabeth had come over to help her paint furniture.

"She and Jeremy drove down to Los Angeles to put in some time at Project Nature there." Elizabeth paused in painting Enid's bookcase. "I don't mind telling you that I'm glad both she and Jeremy are away from Jessica for a while. Things are so tense at home that I feel as if I'm going crazy."

"I can imagine," Enid said sympathetically. "Whatever happened to Sue's wedding dress?"

"We saved it not once but twice. After Jessica ripped it, I had to hide in a closet with a flashlight to sew it up," Elizabeth said indignantly.

"Tsk, tsk." Enid shook her head.

"Oh, I forgot to tell you. Jeremy came over for dinner last night, and my parents have offered to have an engagement party for him and Sue. It's for this Friday. Can you come?"

"Sure, I'd love to. Can I help with anything?"

"Well, I'll be helping Mom with the cooking. You and Jessica and Sue can do the decorations, if that's OK with you."

"That'd be fine. How did Jessica react to the idea of the party?" Enid put down her brush and took a sip from her can of soda.

"The usual. Long, mournful sighs, big cow eyes at Jeremy, you know—the whole Romeo-and-Juliet, star-crossed lovers thing."

Enid giggled, but Elizabeth made a face.

"I don't mean to make fun of her—I'm sure she really does feel awful about the whole thing. It's just that she's not really the type to suffer in silence, you know? And I've been so worried that she's going to say something to Sue, or do something drastic to try to call off the wedding. I can hardly sleep at night, wondering when this whole thing is going to explode in Sue's face."

"Gosh, that must be awful."

"I just wish there was some way to get through to Jessica, to make her stop chasing someone who's unavailable. That *Primal Woman* seminar didn't seem to help. Which reminds me, what do you think about us hosting our own seminar, for teenagers? Just for our friends. We could have it at my house. We'll each read *Primal Woman, Woman of Strength*, and come up with some activities. What do you think?"

Enid looked unsure. "Do you really think we're qualified to lead a group like that?"

"It's going to be very casual—we won't charge admission or anything."

"OK, well, I'll think about it."

It's really too bad that Jessica won't give the Primal Woman *doctrines another shot,* Elizabeth thought on her way home from Enid's that afternoon. What else would open her sister's eyes? When she passed the Sweet Valley main library, she had a sudden idea. She parked and made her way toward the microfiche machine, where she paged through recent back issues of *Nature* magazine. *There,* she thought when she found what she was looking for. Half an hour later, she left the library, a sheaf of photocopied pages in her purse.

"Come on in, Jess," Lila said wearily, standing aside to let Jessica in.

"Lila, what's the matter? What's with the emergency phone call?" Jessica stepped into the cool, air-conditioned comfort of the Fowlers' foyer and got a better look at her best friend. "Have you been crying?"

"All night," Lila confirmed bitterly, leading the way upstairs to her room.

"Well, what's up?" Jessica demanded once they were safely in Lila's large powder-blue room. She threw herself across Lila's bed, and Lila collapsed in the wicker easy chair by the window.

"It's Robby," she said brokenly, reaching for a tissue. "He lied to me."

"What?" Jessica gasped. *Wonderful dream man Robby was leading Lila on?* "He doesn't love you?"

"No, it's not that. . . ." Lila sniffled. "He loves me."

"He doesn't want to get serious? He has another girlfriend?"

"No, he wants to go steady, and there's no one else."

"Then what is it, Li?" Jessica persisted.

"He's not rich!" she wailed, curling up into a little ball in her chair and holding the tissue up to her eyes to catch the liquified mascara collecting there.

"He's not a wealthy art student?" The few times she had met him, Robby sure seemed to know a lot about art and culture. . . .

"No, he's an art student all right, but he's not rich. In fact, he's downright poor! He's going to art school on a scholarship." Fresh tears coursed down Lila's face.

"But you've been to his house," Jessica pointed out. "You've sailed on his boat, and driven around in his Lamborghini. Did he steal all those things?"

"No. He borrowed them. It turns out that his father is the executive assistant to a really rich businessman—someone my dad knows. This guy has known Robby since he was a kid, and so when he and his family went to Europe for the summer, he trusted Robby to house-sit and take care of everything. Robby's parents are divorced, and he lives with his dad. And his dad is in Europe, taking care of business for the guy."

"Wow," Jessica breathed. "So he doesn't have a cent, huh?"

"Not to mention the dog . . ." Lila's tears poured out with fresh vigor.

"The dog?"

"That little Scottie I told you about. It turns out it wasn't even his dog!" Lila moaned, and cried even harder.

"Whoa," Jessica said. "He had the dog under false pretenses?"

Lila nodded miserably.

"So what happens now?"

"I told him I never wanted to see him again, that's what!" Lila declared.

Jessica nodded. It was hard to trust a guy who had lied to you.

"I mean, I thought he was so perfect—he was

175

so much like me, but different, in a good way. He was teaching me about art, and we had so much fun together. Then I find out he has no money!"

Frowning, Jessica turned on her back and looked up at the tiny silver stars painted on the ceiling of Lila's room. "Li, would you have been so upset if you'd found out that he wasn't really an artist?" Jessica asked her after a moment.

"What do you mean? You can't fake talent. Remember, I've seen him draw and sketch—he's really good. He's fabulous at it."

"But what if somehow he had faked it—had just told you that to impress you? Would you hate him for it?"

Lila thought for a moment, then took another tissue and blew her nose. "Well, not really, I guess. I mean, I liked the fact that he was an artist, and I loved the portrait that he was starting to do of me, but I guess I could get over it."

"Even though he had lied to you?"

"Yeah, I guess. I would understand why he wanted to impress me." Lila's expression grew a bit more cheerful. She smoothed her dark hair. "I know I intimidate a lot of guys. I'm gorgeous, I have tons of money. . . ."

"Let's get back to the point for a second here, gorgeous," Jessica interrupted. "First, let's look at the facts. One, Robby is gorgeous. Two, he's totally crazy about you. God knows why. Three, you al-

176

ways have a great time together. Four, he's really talented. Five, all of your friends like him, and he likes all of your friends."

"What are you trying to say, Jessica?"

"I'm saying that what's bugging you isn't the fact that he lied—it's the fact that he has no money." She sat back on her heels. *I'm an absolute genius when it comes to other people's romantic problems.*

Lila frowned. "So what? I'm right back where I started. He has no money! I can't go out with him!"

Jessica stared at her best friend. "You mean you seriously would not go out with that hunkalicious babe simply because you have more money than he does? Good grief, you're an even bigger snob than I thought!"

"He doesn't have *less* money than me," Lila explained impatiently. "He has *no* money. None."

"Who's been paying for everything?"

"Him, mostly. He's getting paid for house-sitting, and he's been saving up. But I pay for some things. We sort of take turns."

"Do you think he likes you for your money?" Jessica demanded. "Do you think he's taking advantage of you?"

Lila thought for a moment. "No," she said slowly. "I haven't picked up on anything like that from him."

"Lila," Jessica said firmly. "Trust me—I know.

177

True love is just too rare a thing to throw it away because of a little hitch in your plans. Robby is a great guy who adores you, and you're ready to dump him for something that's really—let's face it—superficial. I think you're crazy. I mean, look at me. Do you have any idea how thrilled, how ecstatic, how walking-on-air I would be if the only thing keeping me and Jeremy apart was money? It would be heaven!"

Lila got up and walked to her window and played with the curtains. "I don't know," she said. "Money is important."

"Uh-huh. So thank goodness one of you has some," Jessica said dryly. "Li, what if the situation were reversed? What if you were poor and Robby were rich? How would you feel if he dumped you because you didn't have any money?"

"That's totally unthinkable, Jessica," Lila said.

"What's unthinkable is that you're letting him get away."

"What about you and Jeremy? What if you were engaged, and Jeremy came along? Would you break your engagement, like you want him to?"

Jessica didn't even need to think. "In a split second."

"What if you were engaged to Sam?" Lila asked softly.

For a few moments, Jessica felt an almost unbearable sadness wash over her. Then she set her jaw firmly. "Yes, I think I would. Even Sam."

"Wow," Lila breathed.

"There you are," Elizabeth said, coming up to where Jessica was lounging in a chair by the Wakefields' pool. "I've been looking all over for you."

"Is it my turn to set the table?" Jessica mumbled, keeping her eyes shut against the late-afternoon sun.

"Yeah, but that's not what I wanted to tell you. Look."

Jessica blearily opened her eyes to see Elizabeth holding out some papers at her. "What's this?"

"Just look at it."

Sitting up straighter, Jessica took the papers from her sister and began to read. "'Comparative Rates of Destruction Among South American Countries,'" she read. Then her eyes opened wide as she saw the byline. "'By Jeremy Randall and Sue Gibbons.'" She looked up at Elizabeth. "Where did you find this?"

"At the library. Sue had mentioned that they had written some articles together, and I was curious."

Jessica stared down at the photocopy and quickly skimmed the first page. Then she set it down in her lap and looked away. Suddenly she pictured Jeremy and Sue back in New York, working together, living near each other, having dinner parties with mutual friends. All their friends accepted them as a couple. Everyone at their office. They shared a whole world together, a whole world in which Jessica Wakefield had no part.

"You copied this just to show me, didn't you?" she asked Elizabeth calmly.

Elizabeth sat down next to her and looked into Jessica's eyes, so like her own. "Yes," she admitted. "I guess I just wanted to show you how serious they are. Jeremy may not be head-over-heels in love with Sue, but they have a great deal in common and know each other really well. Can you say the same?"

Jessica looked away, biting her lip.

Elizabeth continued, "I know you're in a lot of pain right now, but have you really considered how Sue will feel if she and Jeremy break up? She hasn't felt secure since her mother died. With Jeremy she has a chance to make a new life for herself, make her own home. What will you have if they break up? Let's say Jeremy even moves out here to work in Los Angeles. What about your school? What about college?"

When Jessica looked down at her hands, Elizabeth gently went on. "What do you think his friends would think about his dating a sixteen-year-old? Jess, there are *movies* he wouldn't be able to take you to for a year or two." Leaning over, Elizabeth patted Jessica's hand. "I'm sorry, Jess.

180

I'm not trying to rain on your parade. I want you to be happy. You know that. But I also want you to think this thing through."

Elizabeth stood up and walked quietly back to the house. Jessica stared at the deepening shadows as the sun went down. The breeze made tiny ripples on the pool water. Finally it was almost dark. Soon she had to go in to set the table. But first she dropped her head into her hands and cried.

Chapter 14

"OK, now, how many white balloons did you want?" Jessica asked Elizabeth on Friday morning. It had been a long miserable week. She had seen Jeremy only twice, and only very briefly, and never alone. Now it was the day of the party, and she was doing her best to not fall into a million screaming pieces.

"Uh, I think about twenty-five," Elizabeth said. She was sitting on the Wakefields' living room floor, blowing up peach-colored balloons.

"Ugh," Sue complained from where she was blowing up pale green balloons on the couch. "I feel dizzy."

"Take a little break," Enid advised. She was busily tying balloons together in multicolored bunches with long white curling ribbon. "Actually, Sue, would you mind getting us some drinks?"

183

"I'd be happy to," Sue agreed instantly. "My mouth is parched from blowing up balloons. You guys want some diet Coke?"

Everyone agreed, and Sue headed toward the kitchen, gaily kicking a few balloons out of the way.

"OK, now that she's gone, I wanted to ask you about a bridal shower for her," Enid whispered, leaning toward Elizabeth. "I know your parents are having this party, but I thought a bunch of us girls could also get together and have a shower for Sue."

Elizabeth's eyes shone as she puffed on her balloon. Tying it off, she nodded at Enid. "That's a great idea. You're really nice to think of it. Maybe next week? Or the week after? We don't have much time."

"Well, we might have to have it instead of our *Primal Woman* seminar," Enid said thoughtfully.

Elizabeth nodded. "I'd really like to do both, but I think we'd just end up exhausted."

"Geez, such great choices," Jessica said in an acid tone. "A bridal shower for Sue or Elizabeth's *Primal Woman* seminar. You mean I can't do both?"

"Don't mind Ms. Sour Puss," Elizabeth told Enid. "She's woken up on the wrong side of her bed every morning this week."

"That's a total exaggeration, Eliz—hey!" Jessica's balloon slipped from her hand and sputtered all around the room.

184

Elizabeth and Enid laughed, just as Sue came back in with a tray of soft drinks.

"Thanks, Sue," Elizabeth said.

"No problem. It's the least I can do after all the work you've done this week for the party. All of you." She smiled at all three girls.

Jessica pasted a smile on her face. "You and Jeremy have been really busy this week," she said casually. "I feel as if I've hardly seen you."

"Yeah—we've been working every day at Project Nature in L.A., and Jeremy's there even today. And then at night we've been exploring the great restaurants of Sweet Valley, or going to movies and stuff. I wanted to give your parents a break from having to feed me and entertain us." Sue grinned apologetically as she picked up another balloon and began to blow it up.

"Sue!" Elizabeth exclaimed. "You know they love having you here. We all do. This wedding is the most fun we've had in a long time." Elizabeth tied off her last balloon and patted it through the air toward Enid. "Now, let me see what's next on the list." She consulted a notebook that was lying open on the coffee table. "Did you polish the silver serving dishes?" she asked Jessica.

"Yes ma'am," Jessica said.

"Hmmm . . . we washed the patio furniture. We helped Mom clean the house yesterday. . . . After the balloons we have to arrange the flowers and start some of the food. Who wants to do what?"

"I'll help you make the food," Enid volunteered.

"I can arrange the flowers," Jessica said.

"Good, you're good at that," Elizabeth said, making a mark in her notebook. "Sue, could you take the bunches of balloons and tie them all over the place? Like at the end of the driveway, a few in the house, and a lot of them around the patio in the backyard?"

"Sure thing," Sue said promptly. "This is so much fun—I can't tell you how much Jeremy and I appreciate this party. And I can't wait to meet all your friends." Spontaneously Sue reached over to hug Elizabeth, and then Jessica. Then, laughing, she hugged Enid, too. "This is going to be the best engagement party ever!" she declared, scooping up some balloons before heading outside.

"She's really nice," Enid remarked when she had gone.

"Too nice," Jessica muttered. "It's unnatural."

Elizabeth just laughed at her sister. "What are you going to wear tonight, Jess?"

"I don't know," Jessica said glumly. "I really need a new dress, but I haven't been able to find anything."

"Maybe after you finish the flowers you can go to the mall," Elizabeth suggested.

Jessica shrugged. "Yeah, maybe."

"So is Lila coming tonight?" Enid asked.

"Uh-huh." Jessica smiled slyly. "And of course Robby is too, since he's Jeremy's good friend."

"Hmmm. Do you think she and Robby will get back together?" Elizabeth asked.

"They sure *should*. Robby's really good for her. And it was so nice to not hear her whining about how there was no one around to date."

"Hmmm, that sounds suspiciously like someone else I know," Elizabeth teased.

"Who's that?" Jessica said, throwing down her white balloon and heading for the kitchen before Elizabeth could answer.

Elizabeth sighed. "I've convinced myself that if we get through this party tonight without any major disasters, then Jeremy and Sue will get married without a hitch, so to speak."

Enid giggled. "So to speak. But you said that Jessica had been good all week."

"Mopey, but good. At least that I know about. Who can tell what she's been doing secretly? But Jeremy and Sue have been seeing each other every evening, as well as working together all week. They seem as if they're OK."

"I can't help feeling sorry for Jessica," Enid admitted. "I would feel awful if the one person I loved was engaged to marry someone else."

"I know—but with Jessica, it's always so hard to tell what she's really feeling, as opposed to what she's convinced herself she's feeling.

Anyway, enough about her. What are you wearing tonight?"

"Do you think a silk pantsuit will be dressy enough?"

"Oh, it sounds gorgeous. I'm going to wear my pink flowered sundress, the one with the crossed straps in back."

"That'll be really cute," Enid approved. "So did you talk to Todd yesterday?"

"Uh-huh. He called really late, but I was waiting by the phone."

"Sooo devoted," Enid teased.

"Well, I haven't seen him in over a month!" Elizabeth defended herself, laughing.

"Do you feel better about him, and about, you know, guys in general?"

"I think so." Elizabeth nodded. "At any rate, I definitely feel ready to see him again. I want to start having some fun this summer!"

"Yeah, too bad you've had only my boring, unfun presence so far," Enid said with a mock hurt expression.

Elizabeth threw a pillow at her, and Enid fell over, giggling. "Enid! You know that's not what I meant!"

Laughing, the two friends started throwing balloons at each other.

I have to admit, I have never looked so hot, Jessica mused as she checked out her reflection just before the party. Only an hour and a half before, she had found the perfect outfit at Kiki's, one of her favorite exclusive boutiques. The check she had given them would probably bounce sky high, since paying for Bruce's dinner and then the dry cleaning bill for Sue's wedding dress had totally depleted her account. But that was merely an unimportant detail.

She'd piled her golden-blond hair loosely on top of her head, fixed her makeup, and was ready for Operation Jeremy and Jessica. The gist of the plan would be for Jeremy to take one look at her and feel like dying.

"Jessica, could you tie this bow in back, please?" Elizabeth asked, coming through the bathroom door into Jessica's room. "Wow—you look fantastic." She moved closer to admire Jessica's new outfit.

Jessica preened under Elizabeth's gaze. *Well Liz, when you're right, you're right,* Jessica silently agreed with her sister as she looked at her reflection. The pale-green, sleeveless dress cinched at the waist and flowed softly to mid-thigh. The light rayon fabric accentuated her shapely tanned legs.

"You look great too," Jessica told Elizabeth as she tied the sash on her twin's dress.

"Thanks. I just need to French braid my hair, and I'll be done." Elizabeth flashed her a smile and headed back into the bathroom.

Just as Jessica was finishing her makeup, Sue tapped on her door. "Can I come in?"

"Of course," Jessica said, concentrating on lining her eyes.

"Oh, Jessica—you look beautiful. You're going to break some hearts tonight," Sue teased.

Nothing personal, Sue, but I can't help thinking one of them might be yours. Then Jessica felt a stab of guilt. Sue seemed to be a genuinely nice person, sincere and well-meaning and all. But Jessica just couldn't help it. Sue was in the way, and Jessica was faced with losing the love of her life. What choice did she have?

"Jessica, can you help me with this?" Sue held up a single pearl on a gold necklace.

"Sure." Jessica came over and hooked the necklace around Sue's neck, coolly appraising the other girl's outfit. The dress was navy blue with tiny white flowers, and had a demure scooped neckline and floaty sleeves. *Stylish and festive maybe, but not really sexy or knockout*, she thought with satisfaction.

"There you go," Jessica said.

"Thanks." Sue turned to face her. "Oh, and Jessica—" Just then the doorbell rang and her face lit up. "That must be Jeremy! I better go let him in." Sue whirled and left Jessica's room to run downstairs.

"Want to dance, Wakefield?"

A couple of hours into the party, Jessica turned

around from where she was getting herself a glass of punch and found herself facing Bruce Patman's sneering, handsome face.

"I'm Jessica, not Elizabeth," she said snidely. What fun would hanging out with Bruce be if she couldn't tease him about his thing with her sister?

"No kidding," Bruce said in a bored tone. "Want to dance?"

"Why not?" Jessica put down her glass of punch and went into his arms. The music was medium-paced and swingy, and despite her habitual disdain of Bruce, she had to admit he was a good dancer.

"Where's the lovely Ms. Robertson?" Jessica asked lightly as Bruce swung her around.

"Dancing with Egbert." Bruce gestured toward Winston Egbert, the class clown. Over Bruce's shoulder Jessica could see glimpses of other whirling couples: Cheryl Whitman and Martin Bell, Pamela and Winston, Sue and Jeremy. . . .

"If you're that hungry, try some of the hors d'oeuvres," Bruce said sarcastically, following Jessica's gaze to Jeremy.

"Very funny." Jessica frowned.

As the music ended, Bruce gave her a mocking smile, bowed deeply, then left to claim Pamela for the next dance. It was a slow song, and several of the older party-goers moved onto the wooden dance floor that had been set up.

Jessica saw her parents among them, and again Sue and Jeremy took their places among the dancers.

Brushing a wisp of sunstreaked hair out of her eyes, Jessica went inside to the kitchen, where she found Lila picking at some cream-cheese-stuffed snow peas on a tray.

"These things are great," Lila said, popping one into her mouth.

"Elizabeth and Mom were up until midnight last night putting them together," Jessica testified. "So, have you seen Robby yet?"

Turning away, Lila helped herself to a finger sandwich. "Who?"

"Lila, you're being totally pigheaded. Just give him a chance."

"I *hate* it when guys have less money than me," Lila groaned, rinsing her hands in the kitchen sink.

"Lila, that rules out ninety-nine-point-nine percent of America," Jessica pointed out impatiently.

She and Lila headed back out onto the patio, where Mrs. Wakefield's rose garden scented the soft summer night air.

Jessica spotted Robby across the patio, talking to Jeremy and Sue. *How convenient.* She linked her arm through Lila's and casually wandered over there.

"Let me go, Jessica," Lila hissed, trying to pull her arm away.

"Hi, Robby," Jessica said brightly. "Lila's been looking all over for you."

"You look beautiful, Lila," Robby said quietly. "But then, you always do."

"Wouldn't you like some more peas, Jess? I'll go get some some." But Lila made no move to go. The band started playing a sweet, slow song, and Jessica pushed Lila closer to Robby. "Why don't you guys dance? This is a great song."

Lila stood stiffly, and Robby stepped closer, gathering her into his arms. Jessica watched as they melded with the other dancers. After a few long moments, Lila looked up into Robby's eyes and her body became less stiff in his arms. Soon her head was on his shoulder and he was holding her tenderly as they danced. Once Lila caught Jessica's eye, and gave her a tiny smile.

"Thank goodness that's taken care of," Jessica said.

"You're such a romantic, Jessica," Sue said with an approving smile. "You're a good friend to make sure they got back together."

Jessica felt Jeremy's burning gaze on her. "Life's too short to be without the one you love," she said, watching the dancers.

"Elizabeth!" Sue beckoned to her from the crowd. "It's a great party, isn't it?"

"It seems to be going well," Elizabeth said, coming over with her glass of punch. "But it's such a happy occasion." She gave Jessica a pointed glance. "I wanted to tell you guys to stay close, because I think Mom's going to give you a toast soon."

"Oh, gosh," Sue said with a nervous giggle. "It's nerve-wracking being the center of attention." She leaned closer to Jeremy and put her arm around his waist.

"This is such a pretty song," Jessica said, turning her back so she wouldn't have to watch this revolting display. "It's always been one of my favorites."

"You know, Jeremy likes this song too. You two should dance together," Sue said, disentangling herself from him. "Go on." She gently pushed him at Jessica.

Jessica could almost hear her sister's mental message: *Say no. Say no.* But she looked into Jeremy's night-dark eyes, and as if in a dream they moved closer to each other.

Then everyone else faded from sight as they moved together with a sigh and began to slowly dance to the rhythmic, romantic music.

"You look beautiful," Jeremy said in a choked voice. "But you must know that. You chose that dress for me."

"Yes." *Of course he knew. He understood.* Her heart bursting with a bittersweet happiness, she closed her eyes, relishing the feel of his arms around her, feeling their bodies swaying together to the music. All of Elizabeth's hard facts, even the

Nature articles she'd shown her, seemed completely insignificant. All Jessica knew was that she loved this man and he loved her, and they were dancing closely in the soft, warm air of a beautiful summer evening.

"I've been watching you all evening. That Bruce guy came with someone else. Why did you dance with him when he treats you so badly?"

Jessica stifled a laugh. "Bruce and Pamela have been dating for months. I went to dinner with him that night only to make you jealous. Buying his way was part of the bribe—and he ordered all the most expensive things on the menu." Leaning her head against Jeremy's broad shoulder, Jessica giggled softly. She'd suffer a million dinners with Bruce, a million filet mignons, as long as she could have this moment in Jeremy's arms.

"It worked," Jeremy said, dancing her a little bit away from the rest of the crowd. "I wanted to kill him that night when I saw you smiling at him, eating off of his fork. You made me crazy."

Jessica was suddenly sad again. "But it doesn't really matter, right? You're still going to marry Sue."

"Shh. Don't think about it." Jeremy whirled her in gentle circles until they were far away from the crowd, over by the other end of the swimming pool. The music was growing fainter, the crowd almost invisible. "Jessica, I want to be alone with you," Jeremy murmured into her ear.

Still dancing, still with her arms resting on his shoulders, Jessica silently led them around the end of the pool and past a large, overgrown bank of hedges that bordered their property. She and Elizabeth had hidden here when they were children; this is where Jessica had run when something had upset her greatly. Instinctively, though she was a child no longer, she had returned here with the man who was her destiny.

"Jessica, this is wrong," Jeremy groaned, smoothing her hair with his hand.

"How can it be?" she asked, but deep inside she knew what he meant. He thought she was too young for him, but she didn't think so. He thought he was going to marry Sue, but Jessica knew it was impossible. He thought they had nothing in common, but they had the most important thing in common—love.

Jessica didn't breathe as Jeremy slowly lowered his head to hers. An unbearable shiver ran down her spine. Finally she had what she had been longing for: Jeremy to herself, in private, as though they were boyfriend and girlfriend, as though Sue didn't exist, as though they were made for each other and no one else.

"I love you," he whispered right before his lips claimed hers.

"I love you too." She slid her arms up around his neck. Then he was kissing her and she was kissing him back, and it was as tender and tentative and thrilling as a first kiss. Her head was spinning and she could feel his impatient breathing as they held each other tightly.

Dimly, Jessica heard voices from the party. "Jeremy? Where is he? Alice is ready to make a toast." But she clung to him as they kissed in the night, and this time Jeremy didn't pull away.

Bantam Books in the Sweet Valley High series
Ask your bookseller for the books you have missed

SIGN UP FOR THE
SWEET VALLEY HIGH®
FAN CLUB!

Hey, girls! Get all the gossip on Sweet
Valley High's® most popular teenagers
when you join our fantastic Fan Club!
As a member, you'll get all of this really
cool stuff:

- Membership Card with your own
  personal Fan Club ID number
- A Sweet Valley High® Secret
  Treasure Box
- Sweet Valley High® Stationery
- Official Fan Club Pencil (for secret
  note writing!)
- Three Bookmarks
- A "Members Only" Door Hanger
- Two Skeins of J. & P. Coats® Embroidery
  Floss with flower barrette instruction
  leaflet
- Two editions of *The Oracle* newsletter
- Plus exclusive Sweet Valley High®
  product offers, special savings,
  contests, and much more!

Be the first to find out what Jessica & Elizabeth Wakefield are up to by joining the
Sweet Valley High® Fan Club for the one-year membership fee of only $6.25 each
for U.S. residents, $8.25 for Canadian residents (U.S. currency). Includes shipping
& handling.

Send a check or money order (do not send cash) made payable to "Sweet Valley
High® Fan Club" along with this form to:

SWEET VALLEY HIGH® FAN CLUB, BOX 3919-B, SCHAUMBURG, IL 60168-3919

NAME _____
                              (Please print clearly)

ADDRESS _____

CITY_____ STATE _____ ZIP_____
                                                              (Required)

AGE _____ BIRTHDAY_____ / _____ / _____

Life after high school gets even sweeter!

Jessica and Elizabeth are now freshman at Sweet Valley University, where the motto is: Welcome to college – welcome to freedom!

Don't miss any of the books in this fabulous new series.

♡ College Girls #1 ....56308-4 $3.50/4.50 Can.
♡ Love, Lies and Jessica Wakefield #2........56306-8 $3.50/4.50 Can.